First published in Great Britain in 2025 by
Peirene Press Ltd
The Studio
10 Palace Yard Mews
Bath BA1 2NH
www.peirenepress.com

Jernlungen
Copyright © Kirstine Reffstrup
All rights reserved

First published by Forlaget Oktober, 2023
Published in agreement with Oslo Literary Agency

This translation © Hunter Simpson, 2025

ISBN 978-1-916806-04-7

The translation of this work was supported
by a grant from the Danish Arts Foundation

Danish Arts
Foundation

Designed by Orlando Lloyd
Cover illustration by Magali Cazo
Printed and bound in the United Kingdom by CPI Books Ltd

IRON LUNG

Kirstine Reffstrup

Translated from the Danish
by Hunter Simpson

PEIRENE

IRON LUNG

Here is what I know. I was born two times. First on New Year's Eve, in another city, under another roof in Europe. In the rift between two centuries, I broke the membrane. Twelve strikes and the clocks rang in the new year, time whirred on, the year 1900. I was born in the light between a boy and a girl. I am neither boy nor girl. I drink the bitter waters of the womb. I am far from home, and I sing from this hollow, where I am and am not.

BLEGDAM HOSPITAL
COPENHAGEN, 1952
(August)

The sheets are so white, like soft balls of cotton, like new-fallen snow. The nurses changed them and turned me in the iron lung as the machine sang with my oxygen.

I've been assigned to a wing with the other patients who have contracted the sickness, the night flyers. We have to stay in here, away from the daylight. I close my eyes, flap towards a blinding sun. Most of the sick are children. I'm thirteen years old, neither child nor adult. I pee a long, greenish stream. The urine smells sweetly stale, it flows out of me and spills over the toilet bowl, and though two nurses are there to help me, to support my limp, pliant body, I collapse onto the tiles of the bathroom floor.

The iron lung is long and shiny and cylindrical, and it has hatches on the sides that open up so the nurses can reach me with their hands. The iron lung is longer than I am, it contains all of me, with my soft organs, skin and hair. They push me around on a stretcher that can slip in and out of the iron lung. My body floats inside it like a spaceship. Only my head sticks out of the machine, held in place by a soft white rubber brace.

It's clean and quiet in the big auditorium they roll us into for visitation hours, as if all the footsteps and voices were floating upwards and vanishing under the fans of the ventilator, and all we hear are dogs rooting through the rubbish outside the hospital gates. Chairs line the walls, where the visitors will sit and look on at us with sympathetic faces. The nurses have applied thick layers of powder to their faces, and, compact mirrors open, they colour their eyebrows like fat, black slugs. They move among us, smooth our sheets, adjust the angular white caps fastened to their hair and caress our faces so we can smell their perfume. They furtively slip on high-heeled shoes, and to me they look like film stars or dancers. If I could walk, I'd try on those shoes. I'd run and leap down the hall. Sometimes I ask them for a hairpin, but it's only an excuse to see their bleached curls come loose. If I'm really lucky, they'll cut a lock for me, and then I ask them to put it on the pillow beside me, and I wait for the daylight to hit the hair just right, so the blonde strands shine like a thousand mountain crystals in the sun.

They say the sickness is called polio. A strange word, round, dark, moss-grown and rusty, like an old coin. I taste it. The word is mine now. The sickness rushed in like a giant spider, pinned me down and wrapped me up with its fine, white threads. It lives in me, and I am cocooned in its web. They write it in my journal: poliomyelitis, spreading, attacking my body, mutating it, my brain and my back, the weakened muscles around my lungs, my soft marrow, the grey cells slowly wasting away.

The sickness has paralysed my respiratory muscles. Without the machine I can't breathe, without it I would die. I'm dependent on the machine, but I like to think that it, too, has grown dependent on me, this round shell that closes itself around my body, the long night that falls. Lying here on my back, all I can see is the big, white ceiling, and Ella when she bends down to kiss me. The machine is the prettiest green colour, so shiny that visitors can see themselves reflected in it.

The mechanisms of the iron lung are hidden from me, yet I feel I know it as well as my own body. The machine breathes for me. At the foot is a big leather membrane with a pump that's driven back and forth by a motor. The doctors say that the pump changes the pressure inside, which makes my lungs expand, forces my body to breathe.

Mechanics come with big carts and tools, little cans of oil, and they adjust and calibrate the machine under the watch of the doctors. They check the length of the stretcher, test the membrane, polish the little dials. They kick up dust into my watering eyes. They hold up the membrane in front of the window so that sunlight shines through it, and they rub it down with oil until the veins in the leather are visible.

Ella sits so close that I can see her in the little round mirror hanging at a diagonal above my face.

Ella, sister of flesh and blood.

Ella can drop by the hospital whenever she pleases, and when she's free from school she buys me pears and fizzy drinks, bags full of comic books and Tampax. Then she smuggles my bloody tampons out again so the nurses won't see them. I'm ashamed of the blood. Ella comes every day. I'll always take care of you, she tells me, but can I count on that?

In the first days of the sickness, when Ella couldn't come near me because of the risk of contagion, she watched me through a little glass porthole in the door. I lay all alone in a room. A big room, with open windows and sunlight streaming through light curtains. Mother was there holding my hand, but when they finally opened up the door and led Ella in to me, when she appeared in the diagonal mirror over the iron lung, her voice and her scent flowed through me like sweet milk.

Before I got sick, I breathed freely with my school bag on my back. My footsteps were long and impatient on the hot asphalt. My shoulders were broad and strong. In the purple smog, the cold of winter, with my nose red and my breath swirling around my scarf, I left my mother and our little yellow terraced house at the edge of the city and ran to my place in school.

Mother raised us with hairbrushes and bobby pins, with soap and skirts and scented creams, with pinches when we slouched. I watched the other mothers pushing prams, their older children running ahead of them on the way to school, a grey fatigue under their skin, dried out by vinegar and brown soap. Floury kisses. Little spiders spun cocoons out of lost time and rage in their bosoms. And then there were those women in the pink and liquor-green advertisements in Mother's glossy magazines, holding up powdered detergents and lunchboxes. The big new shiny machines they operated in the kitchen. Siemens. Bosch. I knew I'd never be like them. I sucked in learning, lived among books. I fell asleep at my desk with books open wide, woke up with one hand in a book and the other between my thighs, rubbed and rubbed until my body shook like a rattlesnake, wet and warm, and drew another greedy breath. Spit dripping from the corner of my mouth, strands of white toothpaste across my face, I fell asleep again – one hand in the world of words, the other in dreams.

Now the mattress is hollowed, imprinted with my body, the sheets stiff and crackly as paper. The bare necessities: a glass of water, a notebook, Ella's ears and hands.

Ella is Mother's messenger. Ella carries little notes back and forth between us when Mother can't come herself because she's at work, because she has to provide for the both of us. That's what she always says. Provide. A strange word that makes me think of sadness. We're on our own. My two little goslings, Mother says as she cries. My little wild animals.

We write: *Today is 13 August.*
   I, Agnes, am doing well,
   It smells like chlorine in the hallway.
   The nurses rolled me into a glass room to examine me.
All the children who could walk stood outside, looking in at me.

We write: *I hate margarine.*
   Mother writes: *Eat peas instead.*

I can't use my hands, I can only lift my left one and move it a little, and I need help with everything. With washing myself, with eating. I have to lie completely still in the iron lung with my arms at my side while my body is pumped with air and the nurses swarm around me like great white butterflies, feed me pale pear pudding, little biscuits and soft, canned peaches. I can hear the wind in the chestnut trees outside, the leaves in the treetops rustling like snake-skins as it blows through them.

I ask:
   Ella?

Am I very sick?
Will I have to stay here forever?

Ella takes my hand, squeezes it. She shakes her head:
Are you hungry? Should I get you some juice?

I answer:
Stay a little longer. Don't go.

Ella gave me a white lizard. Dry and shrunken, flat, bleached by the sun. Its little eyes were punctured, only black dots in the white, and I looked at its tiny, humanlike hands as Ella rotated the reptile in the sunlight. Its hands were spread out in the air, as if the animal were reaching for me or trying to tell me something in a silent, secret sign language. Its skin felt rough. It glittered. Ella took it out of her pocket at the Bellahøj fairgrounds, and she showed it to everyone in line for the carousel, like some strange, ghostly prize. She put the lizard under my pillow, and right away my dreams were different, suffused with a calm light. The light came from deep inside a mountain of salt, where a pink lantern shone through the crystals, and I curled up and fell asleep at the foot of the mountain and dreamed within the dream of another sleep, as the mountain exuded its dizzying fairground fragrance of raspberry and candyfloss.

The nurses fasten their white caps with bobby pins and walk briskly down the hallways. I inhale the same air as them. They eat and sleep in the building beside the epidemic ward. They are bound to me by an invisible ribbon. My sickness makes it possible for them to fulfil their duties. The building wraps itself around them, organizes their thoughts and habits for them. They walk back and forth between their beds and ours through long, gleaming hallways. They pick little puffballs of fear out of our sleep. They give us bread porridge and ether-soaked sponges, laugh with us, they tickle us with feathers from their blankets, bend over us and take our hands and tell us about the parties they went to when they were on leave, about their boyfriends and families, tampons and tonic water for pimples, their little apartments far from the city centre, in Amager, Nørrebro and Nordvest. They share their secrets with us, about the boyfriends and lovers who pick them up on bicycles, drop condoms and little notes written on wax paper into their uniform pockets. *Never leave me. Come back tomorrow and give me a thousand kisses.*

I ask the nurses: What's the matter with me?

They say: Don't cry. Soon it won't hurt any more. Take this little pill.

I ask for the nurse I like the best, with the dark, curly hair and the deep voice and a pocket full of pink chewing gum that she secretly doles out to us children: Can you hold my hand for a little while?

The head nurse with little glasses and a black band around her white cap pushes me back and forth on the metal plate that holds the soft mattress where I lie. She opens the hatches on the sides and says: How are you today? Where does it hurt? She touches me with her warm hands, adjusts the pressure in the machine. My own arms are soft as milkshakes from lack of use. She rolls the iron lung beneath a window as I asked her to, so the wind from outside can blow across my face, tickle me with its microscopic grains of sand, and so I can, for an instant, when I close my eyes, imagine I'm not a night flyer but that I'm walking around out there, upright, in the blinding light of day.

The nurses carry a television into our room to cheer us up. It's in a rectangular box, the television's big grey eye on top and the speaker below. The television is a sensation throughout the ward, and nurses and porters come in and sit on the floor, gather around it alongside the patients. They turn the mirror over the iron lung so I can see the screen too. The pictures flicker, black-and-white silhouettes. The crackling lattice of the speaker sends forth voices and music. The nurses hand out little bags of popcorn that slip from our slack hands. They give me a pill, too, and I take it without complaint.

An announcer lady presents the next broadcast, from America. The screen flickers like it's on fire.

The announcer lady says that the USA has carried out the first observations of live monkeys and mice in a state of weightlessness during ballistic launches over White Sands, New Mexico. They have now succeeded in sending a monkey into space and back to earth alive. Yorick the monkey was kept company by eleven mice. The animals were all sedated. And one day people, too, will reach the moon.

There's a technical problem and the screen goes dark. At night, the television's eye turns on all by itself. The test pattern lights up, I can see it in the mirror. I lie awake and stare at the screen's snow.

I think of the monkeys, confused and drunk on anaesthesia, tied into an iron seat with their helmets on. They see the earth's spherical form, the sky-blue earth, the formations of the clouds. Time moves more slowly out in space, but they can't feel the difference. They see the world from the outside, a ball they wish they could reach. They eat bananas and cornflakes, and the banana peel floats through the air.

Ella.
Sister.
Have you heard of the monkeys in outer space?
Do you think I'll ever get out of here?

When Mother comes, she shuffles in quietly and bends over the iron lung as if it were a coffin. She always arrives just before noon, having pedalled through the city from the office, bearing the city's restless motion with her, the whine of the tram, footsteps and shouts and whirling dust. Stripes of hair stick to her sweaty skin. Sunlight sits on her forehead, shining like a pad of butter. She can only stay for her lunch break. I stare at her as she places cloying chocolates on my pillow and drapes soaked, checked handkerchiefs over my face if I'm too hot.

I breathe heavily through the cool, wet fabric.

Mother used to serve us dinner in the late afternoon. We sat in the dining room, scraped the sauce from our plates, hair falling over our eyes, over shiny, pimply skin. The big Moroccan rug swallowed every sound, swallowed the sputters of the radio, which was always on, even when it broadcast nothing but a misty hum. The curtains slid down to the floor like snakes and threatened to strangle us. Mother would light a cigarette, put her feet up, and we'd drum our fingers on the tabletop. She never left us alone. She would knock on our bedroom door, leave her shoes right outside it to remind us that she was still there, still watching over us whenever we cracked it open. And now there she is in the mirror above me. Restless, flicking lint from her blouse, crinkling the cellophane of her King of Denmark sweets.

Agnes.
Agnes, it's me.
My girl.

Mother says: Do you get enough to eat here?
I answer: When are you coming back?
Mother says: Ella will come and see you tomorrow.

She bends over me, reaches her hand in through the hatch. Her hand crawls over my body, feeling every tendon, every muscle. As if she wants to reassure herself that I'm still alive. Her hand weaves itself into my hair. She laughs nervously and says: I've got to get used to it here. It's so different, Agnes. So white, so cold. Agnes, you're handling it all so well. She pulls a cigarette from the pack in her pocket and the smoke flows softly into the room, wraps itself around her head until it almost vanishes in restless, blue waves of nicotine. I sniff at it greedily, because it reminds me of home. The ember of the cigarette is a little insect flitting around Mother. She rests her hand between my breasts to make sure I'm getting enough oxygen. Her own breathing is silent. Her hand rises and falls with my breathing. The big hands of the electric clock in the room quiver. Silently they whir.

I wait for a sign, wait for the ceiling to split open with a deafening blast, for the white plaster to spread like a mountain chasm, for the mortar to crumble down into my eyes, to fall over all the patients, to fall over the children like snow.

A sign that Mother will bring me home again.

But she leaves every time, leaves me here alone.

I'm thirteen and a half today. The machine is my armour, and I'm a little Joan of Arc. The pyre burns, eats away at my bones.

Ella says: They broke into our house. It was because of the risk of contagion. Mother stood at the door and blocked their way, they had to move her by force.

Ella saw it all through the crack in our bedroom door. They went through each room and Mother reluctantly pointed out my belongings. They taped the doors shut. They burned everything I'd touched, everything that had come into contact with my body. Poetry books, school bags, summer dresses and winter coats, pants and shoes, sheets and even the bed I slept in, they carried it out into the garden and set it on fire. The fire burned high. The smoke spread softly across the sky.

It was in July. The sickness had arrived. It was among us. Among the children. A soft, blue shadow clung to our backs. The summer slipped away from us like fine white sand. The bright nights, the sky wide open day and night. Only distantly, in the anxious whispers of adults, from the hissing radio, did we hear of the epidemic that had hit the country. The grown-ups said: There's a plague among the children. The grown-ups said: Stay close to me. We heard the sirens from Blegdamsvej. We saw the lines of ambulances. But we drove the other way, to the beach.

The sun was big and white. We'd just been in the water, Ella and I. I walked around with pockets full of amber and the most beautiful light, flat beach stones that I skimmed across the water. In the grass lay a handkerchief, a fine, white handkerchief: Look what I found. I picked it up and showed it to Mother. Mother said: Get rid of it, hurry. A few days later I caught a cold, or that's what Mother thought. My legs hurt, I felt a hot malaise. I had an errand to run for Mother. To buy a quarter-block of ice for the icebox. I stepped in between the cracks in the pavement. The air in the shop was cool and blue, the tiles smooth. Fresh milk, butter in barrels, big round blocks of cheese, eggs. A cellar smell in the middle of summer. I had coins in one pocket and beachstones in the other. I

25

wanted so badly to buy a bottle of the thick white milk
with the change, but Mother had told me not to. I drank
a bottle anyway, and the milk ran heavy down my chin. I
licked away my milk moustache. The clerk blinked, took
off his glasses. My chest was glazed with summer sun.
He stared at my legs, and for a few seconds my thighs
were his. He chopped the ice block apart with a pick.
I turned with the bottle and the ice and left, took wide
steps, dropped the glass on the asphalt. A beam of light in
every shard. The shards crunched under my feet. I walked
and walked and the road grew soft, tugged at my feet,
stretched itself out before me. A terrible pain, a white
spot in the middle of my forehead. My legs felt heavy.
There was a buzzing in my knees, in my hips, in my chest.
I felt dazed. I wanted to walk, but I couldn't. I had to
keep rubbing the beachstones in my pocket to stay calm.

Then I fell to the street. Suddenly I was so light, and the
road beneath me was soft velvet. I lay on the asphalt and
looked up at the hazy summer sky. For an instant all the
people were insects whirling around me, and they stopped
to look down at me from above. Then the air and sky
were empty. The dust floated. I blinked. Everything was
bright. I gasped for air. I walked through a landscape of
chalk-white stone and shells I'd had in my pocket, washed
up on land, washed round and clean by the sea, and I
climbed over the great marbled shells and white stones. I
saw ribbons of strong, bright colours, sparklers and glittering planets gliding endlessly across my retinas. Then I
heard the sirens.

Agnes?

Can you hear us?

You've been asleep a long time.

Agnes, can you tell us who you are and where you live?

Ella says that the ambulance drove me up Blegdamsvej. To the epidemic ward. They revived me with a mix of oxygen and ammonia. They undressed me and took a spinal tap with a long, sharp needle. A nurse held me as if in an embrace as they stuck the needle in. A long, piercing pain. Within one day the paralysis spread to my legs and arms, then to the muscles in my chest. I lay completely still, blue from lack of oxygen. Then they lifted me into the iron lung.

I am a night flyer, but Ella came in a cloud of raspberries and deep-fried food, smelling like the day smells. Ella bent over me, and my voice sounded so thin, she said, as if it came from the machine, as if it was the machine's own squeaking sounds. Death sat on the bedpost, as thin and green as a neon tube, tiny and glowing, shrivelled. He rattled a ring of keys and puffed himself up, making a mockery of me. But then I saw Ella, and his face went pale at her laughter, dissolved and disappeared. Agnes, look what I have, Ella said. She refused to leave the hospital until I awoke. She brought chewing gum and movie tickets for me, soap shaped like crystals to cheer me up. The moment I saw Ella, I started to speak. And now I'm telling what I saw.

When I fell to the asphalt, the old world disappeared. The world I knew with Ella and Mother, the hot asphalt and July sun.

I saw a fire. I saw it with my eyes and with the eyes of others. I saw it from deep within, as if from the bottom of a well, and I watched the people around me from the outside. I saw their habits and their lives, how they washed their hands and moved through time as if through a deep valley. Maybe I wasn't myself. Maybe I was many people with many eyes. I had neither form nor face. Maybe I was just sensory nerves, folds of skin and pupils. I looked up into an empty room. It was misty at first, with waves of bluish fog and a feeling of eternity. I couldn't see clearly, and every time I tried, black worms danced before my pupils. I whisper to Ella that I think I've lived another life, that it was that life I saw.

I was somewhere I've never been before. In a city I've only read about in books. The city was called Budapest. I floated over the rooftops, across the river. The sun was rising, and it had rained that night. The rooftops and the low mountain ranges had a greenish lustre. That was one image, and in the next my body hung above another body, naked, lying asleep in a bed. It was a woman. There was a strong stench of sweat in the room, of soot, of toxic amniotic fluids. The wallpaper was peeling, the sheets yellow. The woman cried in her sleep. A greenish fluid dripped from between her legs. She was pregnant, her belly bulging and marbled with blue. I was right above the woman, as if held aloft by an invisible current of air. She was waking up. I was only a few centimetres from her, so close I could touch her skin and see behind her flickering eyelids, then my body sank further down, meeting no resistance, and the body, my body, hung there in the air, just above and a little to the side of the other, who devoured hours of sleep, no thoughts of the past or the future in the circular turbine of dreams.

The woman turned onto her side. She was alone, and she was in labour. It came from deep within. Something grew, layer upon layer of flesh and tendon and muscle folding and extending, and the little heart at the very centre pushed itself through her cervix. Then she awoke, arched her body in the bed, working towards the pressure and the pain. She turned on her side and threw up, streams of soft, green vomit.

And now her body opened. Her pelvis melted away, loosened, cartilage and bone giving way. A little dome of skull became visible, curly hair, a tuft of darkness pasted to the scalp.

A midwife in a long black gown came into the room. She bent down and pulled the child's head, tugged at the little shoulders, which were stuck. She turned the birthing woman. She massaged the opening and the folds of purple, blue and white mucous membranes, pulled, pushed, kneaded and yelled at the woman. She opened a bag full of bottles and boiled, sterilized instruments, and finally she cut through into flesh, through the membranes and fat that folded out into a bloody wreath, until the child broke through and the head slipped out, crowned with fat and shit and amniotic fluid.

The midwife turned the child over, examined it, spread its legs, touched its genitals with a thumb and sighed. She cleaned its eyelids and its sex with a little sponge. She weighed and measured the child and wrote the numbers down, as she had been instructed to do when she helped unmarried women. She whispered to it and sang:

> *Little child*
> *Be strong.*
> *The clock rang right over you.*

Time received you on a New Year's Eve.
I've never seen such a beautiful, strange child.
You are the first of your kind
and the last.
You are growing in a new century.

The midwife bent over the little newborn, cut the umbilical cord and tied it, gathered up the placenta, wiped away the blood, put it all into a bowl and carried it out.

I reached out my hand. I saw my own birth. It really was me. My skin shone white with vernix. It beamed from me, from all my features. The blind, milk-white eyes were mine. Those little hands, flapping through the air in that room in Budapest, were mine. The quiet sobs. The mouth that opened like the yawn of a baby bird. Everything was mine. Time, standing before the child like a gleaming pillar. The wrinkled forehead.

The mother woke in a daze, sedated with morphine and ether, and found the child by her side. She looked at it. She cried. She kissed the child. She licked it clean. She was hungry and she chewed at the little stump of umbilical cord that remained, bluepurple, gnarled. She pulled and sucked it from the baby's skin, licked away the remnants of blood and vernix around its mouth. Then the mother fell asleep again, and when she awoke after several days, she swaddled the child, pulled on her coat, left the house and carried it down to the river.

Big flakes of snow were beginning to fall. She shivered. The water flowed gently. She turned her face to the sky and snowflakes floated into her eyes. Snow, she whispered to herself. The strange, chemical smell of new-fallen snow. She bent down, unwrapped the child from the fabric and washed it carefully in the river. She filled her palm with ice-cold water and poured it over the child's head. It started screaming wildly. Its skin flamed red and blue. The shiny little eyes fluttered and looked up at her. She laid the child down on the riverbank and vomited again, porridge mingling with the waters as the child cried and flailed in the cold blanket of white. Then she put the child to her breast and tied it there. She walked along the river, out of the city. The water's reflection billowed and blinded her. Snowflakes melted against her skin. The water sang magnetically, tugged at her, glossy, metallic. As she walked along the river, everything became lighter. The weight of the child and the strange dark heaviness in her body abated. She took short steps. One step at a time, and the child grew calm. Now she walked towards the forest. She walked towards Tara's house.

TARA'S HOUSE, 1913

(the boys)

I am the child the mothers cast away.
I breathe down through the century.

I live in the big house. Here my body has grown long and slender, and above my lip grows a soft down, which I stroke with my index finger. The house has many rooms. The rose-coloured wallpaper in the parlour is damp and dimpled. The walls are silent. The walls listen. I don't know how long I've been in the house. Tara says that I'll be thirteen years old this year, that I've been here for thirteen years. I've grown up among the boys. I remember: snow, shadows, the boys' eyelids, which turn purple when they sleep.

The house lies at the edge of the forest. Beside the house flows the river, bending and running south, where the insects hatch. In the garden there grow acacias, walnut trees and great, knotty oaks, whose long, thick roots arc and weave themselves across the ground. Behind the garden begins the forest. We can see the tops of the birch trees swaying in the wind. We can see the fog coming through the tree trunks like the white, unknown ocean in which we've never swum. Behind the forest we can see the mountains. And on the other side of the forest, far away from us, lies the city. The river is the Danube. They call the city Budapest.

Tara inherited the house. She lives here with her sister Maria and us. The sisters take care of us, watch over us, the abandoned children. Our eyes are shiny coins. Lonely alms cups. Our bones and tendons grow long, our wounds deep. Knots of cartilage, growing flesh, layer upon layer of fat. Our hair, cut above our ears and straight across our foreheads, hangs down our necks. Tara calls us: *My warriors*. The sisters raise us, clothe us with clothes they've sewn themselves: a shirt with a high, stiff, cylindrical collar, a pair of brown trousers with soft lining, a blue summer jacket, and a grey woollen coat with a fur collar for the cold months. We roll the trousers halfway up our shins. The jackets have wide trumpet sleeves. Maria sewed them with three silk strips and the word *home* embroidered on the sleeve with pink thread, so people will know where we come from if we ever run away.

My face is like the house. It, too, has many rooms. It opens and closes depending on who is looking at it. It changes with the light, the night and the day. And between my eyes the brows have grown together, like one of the dark insects that flit below the ceiling in the summer and sit on the inside of the windowpane – a night flyer.

It was Tara who opened the door of the house and picked me up. A blind bundle, bald eyebrows, all white with vernix. You looked up at me with your crumpled and nearly newborn face, Tara says, such a strange face, quivering, the skin red and soggy. Tara swaddled me in clean sheets and held me to her breast, sprinkled baking soda on my skin to suck up the vernix. My umbilical cord was gone and it had left a deep wound. She stuck a needle in my side to see how loud I would scream. She pressed a bandage to the wound where my umbilical cord had been, where the blood still pulsed strongly. She rubbed me with salt from the big tub in the parlour to clean me. She examined me. Who are you? she asked. I looked so strange. I wasn't made like other children. But my gaze clung to her, made it impossible for her to say no. My eyes were two shiny little lakes. They fluttered, squinted, beseeched her to hold me tight, not let go. Tara let me live in the house. I was absorbed into the house's order.

Tara says: This is a home for boys.

But I am not like the other boys.

Tara says: We've never had anyone but boys here.

But I am a stray insect.

She says: My boy. You are my strange boy. And every morning she examines me to make sure that it's true. But I have watched the boys in secret. Oh, I've seen them. Tears in my eyes. Sweat on my palms. Their dangling flesh and two boiled plums when they pull off their trousers at night. I've seen them spray urine and watery milk from that soft rod that rises. Shame on you. One must keep one's fingers over the blanket, Tara says, one must be clean. But my eyes suck up the boys' milk. I have slender wrists and light down over my lip. My sex is smooth and arching like a big goose egg. Sex is a word Tara and the doctors have taught me, but the word does not belong to me. If I touch the egg with my fingertips, I feel a soft fold, and when I rub it with my thumb, my body quivers and I double over, gasping. But I almost never caress it, because Tara says: You must never touch yourself, so I quickly pull my hand away. Tara says: You must never show yourself to anyone but me, and I pull my trousers on. I button my shirt and the stiff, high collar, and the fabric wraps so tightly around my chest, my throat, that the air drains from my lungs and I can hardly breathe.

Tara enforces a strict law: You may never see one another naked. We must have rules, the boys and I, so we don't fall into dissolution. Without Tara we'd be lost. And if we don't adhere to her orders, she puffs herself up, enraged, and her chest swells as big as the stomach of the sheep we killed last summer. But I've begun to look at the boys. I lick my lips. The boys' hips sway. I long so much to see them I could burst.

The house speaks to me at night. I'm not alone. The house settles, its cold zinc pipes sing. The wallpaper creaks and stretches to reach across the walls. The mice wake up and rustle about behind the skirting boards, and the bats hanging from the rafters fling themselves into the darkness. I crouch down, barefoot in the milk cellar at dawn. A chill pounds up through the cold tiles. My white breaths swell, a veil over my mouth. I look into the wooden pails of milk that have been set out to gather cream. A daddy-long-legs flails in a dizzy, confused dance atop the thick milk. There are dead flies caught in its yellow skin, in the pearls of creamy fat. I dip my hands into the tubs and pick out the flies. Tara says that it's not for us to drink, that the milk is for cream and cheese and churned butter, but my pulse beats my body warm and I take what I want. I hold one of the tubs up to my mouth and silently drink until it is empty. The milk bubbles in my mouth, runs thick as oil down my chin and my neck. I lick away my milk moustache, dazed and dizzy.

I tip over one of the tubs, spill the milk across the floor. Now it won't be me but the hounds who've got out of the stable. That's what I'll tell Tara.

Maria has taken out the wooden platters and ladles. Jars line the wall in the half-dark. The peeled aubergines in the

40

glass look like strange organs from the medical experiments Maria shows me photographs of in the newspaper. Swollen grey brains.

I rub the hardened soles of my feet to warm them. I lift the lid of the butter churn, dip my thumb down and drag it through the dripping, dark yellow mass, smear it across my mouth and lick my lips clean. My thumb leaves a cleft in the thick butter.

In the parlour sits the horsehair sofa and the long, shiny oak table where we eat our meals. Empty. Without the boys' voices. The house is splashed with the day's first light, which clings to the carpets, to my pupils. On the wall in the corridor hang great paintings, misty landscapes with gilded frames. In one of the paintings a herd of horses emerges from the fog, their muzzles pressing against the taut canvas as if they were coming towards me with their gigantic, bulging eyes.

Then a key turns, a door in the corridor opens, a strip of light falls in.

A shiver, like when the rain hits me from the sky before I can seek shelter in the house.

Steps in the hall. Quick breathing.

Tara.

Tara's straight back.

Tara's smell of tallow and garlic.

Tara's voice, which fills the hallway even when she whispers.

I've seen your hiding place.

Little child.

I can hear her starting a fire in the kitchen, rattling the fire iron. She sharpens a knife, blade against stone, swish-swish-swish. She calls out from the half-dark as fire rises in the burners. I don't answer. I ball up my hands, back into the wall, a knot in my throat. I hear water trickling. Tara hums and says: If you don't come out, I'll come and get you and throw you into the pot. I know she never means the things she says, except when she's red and fuming because I've driven her mad. But still her words make my body seize up and I tremble like a wounded kid goat, fragile and scared. I whisper to myself in the darkness: I'm coming.

The garlic we harvested late from the garden lies in great bundles on a bench in the kitchen. Tara crushes one clove and braids long garlands and wreaths with the rest. They crackle. Tara grinds her teeth. Tara, standing straight, her unruly grey hair falling over her forehead, though she has plaited it and wrapped it around her head. She wears a long dark linen dress. A high white collar reaches up her neck, the same as we boys have, which gives her a silhouette as tall as a statue. Tara tightens her lips. She stands at the kitchen window in a cloud of fat flies, beside baskets of onions and apples and sides of smoked meat. She grips the knife, clenches her jaw. Her hands burn red and blue from the work. The grey light of morning flows over her face.

There you are. Tara puts the knife down, turns to face me: Take off your clothes. At first, I refuse. No. Tara tempts

42

me: You can be the first to taste the soup. You can set the table. You can have the best, fattest piece of ham. She draws me to her and kisses me, combs her fingers through my hair. I soften against her breast, sink into the fabric, inhale her strong scent of garlic, of the little spiced cigarettes she keeps hidden in a wooden box – Irving Magnolia – guarded by a bison painted blood red. I relent like the thin skin of a plum, splitting against Tara's breast.

Let's have a look at you.
My boy.

Tara pulls off my nightshirt and I stand naked before her. It's as if everything is falling apart. The air feels rough and salty, heavy to inhale. I feel the beating of my heart, the sweat under my arms, and, deep within the dank walls, the beating hearts of the others, the boys, who are fast asleep, and their breathing, which draws the darkness out from under their beds. They don't know I'm standing here. They don't know that I, every morning, hide in the hall or between the great knotty roots of the oak tree. They don't know that Tara hunts me like a little mouse, and that, every morning, she finds me.

A taste of iron fills my mouth, as if I'm spitting blood at the thought that the boys might wake and see me now.

Tara turns me around with her burning hands, around and around. My small nipples stiffen. Sugar breasts, Tara whispers, letting her fingers glide down my ribs, sugar breasts, sugar cubes, these two round swellings that have begun to grow, so small she can pinch them between her fingers. They're practically nothing, she says as I stretch my arms out, her fingers registering every fold of skin, every bone and meandering vein.

Over my belly.

Her hands up between my slender thighs. She grasps my egg, smooth and curved, marbled purple and blue. Tara mumbles: The egg. We must take care of it. She strokes her fingers over it, which makes me dizzy, it swells, big and shiny against her hand, and I turn away in shame at the sight of her flushing face, at feeling her fingers on my skin, and I turn red as a boiled beetroot when I hear her sigh. Tara says: Stay with me always. Tara says: Never show yourself to anyone, that way you can remain Boy here in the house. Tara picks up my shirt, washed clean, stiff and scratchy with soda. She gives me my trousers, helps me button my shirt while I shake, and she keeps going until my chest is wrapped so tight in the clean, white fabric that I lose my breath.

Boy, Maria calls.

Boy, where are you? Tara shouts when she wakes in her bed, fumbling for me between her sweaty sheets.

In this house we have no names. The sisters call me Boy, as if it were a name. Or The Child. Their little insect. I am confused, bewildered. I beg them, I pester them. I want a real name like them. But they say no. Shake their heads. The sisters have no name for me, and I've never been baptized. The sisters say: Once you're old enough, you can have a name. I ask them what it means to be old enough.

They say I'll get a name when I leave the house, and one doesn't leave the house until one is old enough, unless something explodes inside you, breaks, and, against all advisement, you leave the house, cross the border and go off into the forest. A few boys have gone into the forest before they were old enough, and they never came back. They left nothing behind, not even their names.

I show them my contempt, click my tongue, lick my lips, feel the soft, short down above my lip, not like the dark stubble of the older boys. I call myself Milk Moustache, like the one I get after I've drunk a whole tub in the milk cellar, or Bean, like the thin, green pods in the garden that the sisters pluck. Sprouting. Peeled. Exposed to the world.

I set the long table in the parlour, my body full of trembling.

My heart beats against the stiff white fabric of my shirt.

It is the same day, I've pulled the night with me through the hours. I've painted myself a little moustache with coal from the fireplace.

The joy of it.

The fear of it.

The fear, like when the green branches of the acacia tree beat against the windowpane and we think there's a stranger out in the garden.

I want to look like the other boys.

Now you'll see.

It's almost noon.

Twelve strikes from the grandfather clock.

I waver like a spiderweb in the breeze.

I wait for the boys.

The long, bright oak table. Twelve newly polished tin spoons and twelve tin plates, one for each of us. A great bowl of salt. A platter with garlands of garlic. A bowl of vinegar and vase of black, coloured roses in the middle of the table. The salt crystals sparkle. The strong, spicy scent of the flowers makes me dizzy.

Maria opens the door soundlessly, cuts a thin slice of light from the garden and the snow, which covers the grass in a thin layer. She hangs shoots of sage over the door frame. *Contra vim mortis, non crescit herba in hortis*: there grows no herb in the garden stronger than death. Maria cups her hand, wipes the damp and the ashes from the walls with a cloth, tears the spiders from the walls, casts them into the fire, which blazes and makes little pops as they explode.

Maria sits down and holds my hand in hers, her skin so dry, as if turned in flour. Small and slender, the bones loose beneath her skin. Maria is sick, there's a sickness in her lungs, her breath squeaks, whistles through her lips and turns her cheeks blue, her eyes bulging, blinking. She has a chemical smell, like the pills she swallows, like the house's noxious stench of soot and garlic.

Consumption, Tara whispers: soon death will come and take you away from us.

Soon, soon, soon, Maria says with a chuckle. But I'm alive yet.

Lunchtime, Tara calls. She rings a little copper bell. I blink, press my cheek to the rose-coloured wallpaper. The walls murmur. The bell rings again. Then, finally, I hear the boys. They swing open the doors, coming in herds, the younger ones from the yellow room and the older ones from the purple one. The drumbeat of twenty-two legs. They gallop in, slender calves, their light and dark voices filling the corridor.

The older boys sleep in the purple room where the white geese live, and when they lock the door at night, my heart beats so wildly that I think it might pound right through my chest. The geese shriek, and the smell of wet mucous membranes and sweat seeps out under the door, a smell of something forbidden, something terrible. The shouts and screams from in there make us, the littler ones, so scared we hide under our blankets.

I lie in the yellow room every night with the other little boys, though I'll soon be too big and I can already kiss the tops of their heads from above. Everything in there is painted dark yellow: the ceiling and the walls, even the door frames, which sunlight warms in the summertime. Tara says that we're her light, we young ones, whom the morning sun caresses.

Now the boys are here. I've felt alone without them. Shivering, they sit on the sofa and the floor. The younger boys dart around Tara, the elder ones shove each other as if inebriated, shove me so I shrivel like a salted carp and want to hide in a corner until their shouting and raging is exhausted. They button their open shirts with a row of shiny black buttons. Their high, stiff collars reach up to their ears and force their necks straight. The older boys are taller than the sisters, the younger are shorter than me. I do what they do, raise my voice and smooth my trousers. Every day we enact the same ceremony: we bow for the sisters, we shake hands with each other like strangers. I put the napkins on the table, one for each boy, a silver ring around each. The hyacinths on the windowsill eat the dusty air, their noxious blossoms grimacing like heads in a bell jar. Blue and black. The food is ready, Tara calls.

The stew, I skimmed it myself. Fat chunks of meat and onion rings drift on the surface, and the sisters have made kifli, sweet and salty, layer upon layer of yeasty white dough folded into half-moons and placed in the sun to leaven, where they glisten white, strewn with sesame seeds and dead flies. Soon the boys will eat. Soon they will lick the crumbs from their lips, lick my meat stew from their spoons.

Tara gives me the sign, and I say: Take your seats.
   The younger boys shout: Never ever.
   The elder boys say: You'll regret it.

We sit around the table and I sink into the boys' company. Shoulder to shoulder. I become their shadows, their laughter. Their smells of soil and chewing tobacco and smoked meat. Tara circles the table, bending over each one of us, counting us though she knows we're all there. Twelve. She strokes our heads. Her twelve boys, our high collars crackling with starch and soda. The boys sit in rows according to age, with me in the middle. A straight stalk. Tara's mouth hangs slightly open, her breath yeasty. We hold out our hands and Tara inspects our fingernails, hand by hand. She has a little knife in her pocket. We grip the tabletop: the trick is to stay very still as she gouges the filth from under our nails.

Our nails grow.

Dark half-moons.

Filth, says Tara.

We file our nails.

Brittle and bowed.

With our nails we can reach the flies down in the cracks of the floorboards.

With our nails we can scratch each other's cheeks, flay the skin into thin bands.

Sometimes Tara's knife slips under our nails, and we scream, suck up the blood that gushes down our hands in stripes.

When Tara is done with our nails, she takes her place at the head of the table. Maria sits at the other end. They clasp their hands and pray to the forest and the soil for protection, and we whisper: *Give us fruit and meat*. They pray to the house for protection, and we sing: *Hold back the dark*. Then we lift our knives and butter our bread. The sisters eat off porcelain plates, painted with brown landscapes. But they prefer to look at our faces than at the porcelain. We boys, of whom they are so proud. Look, we have such good appetites, we're growing strong. We're getting fat! We grunt, put on a little show for them. Little piglets. We squeal at them and clink our knives on our plates.

Tara rings her bell for the third time, and the hyacinth's wormy roots reach down to the floor, growing fat like white meat, like blanched, supple tendons as Maria serves the stew, as we gulp down the potent fluid, a row of pulsing muscles and breath and restlessness, silver spoons flashing halfway to our mouths. The boys. And I sit among them. We are twelve straight silhouettes against the light.

When the older boys taste the soup, they shout: Meat!

The younger boys whisper: We hate meat.

Then Tara says: There's no more milk. Loudly over the table, she says: Was it one of you?

No more milk, and thus no more cream and no more butter.

This is the last butter.

Save it.

I look down at my plate.

Has she found me out?

No, it resounds within me.

No, it resounds within.

I take a bite of the bread Tara serves, the priceless dark yellow butter, of which there will now be no more, which we must now wait weeks to have again, because the milk has been stolen. I stare at the teeth marks. I beam at the boys with my fat butter-smile. Their hands reach out, their eyes ravenous. Adam's apples jutting. The boys' joy at mealtimes, the light in their eyes, the grease on their lips. Their shoulders, their flat chests heaving and falling beneath their scratchy, clean shirts. I speak in a deeper register, like them. I stick out my throat, like them.

Then they notice my moustache, the thread of soot.

The boys laugh and drum their fingers.

Tara sees it too. Tara says: What have you done? She spits and rattles, rubs the skin above my lip.

The boys laugh. I bow my head.

Nothing.

Silence.

Obstinacy.

Two little mounds under my shirt.

My hands make fists.

The boys glower.

Maria's spoon hangs in the air.

Let him be.

Tara rages.

Tara let me into this house, and now it's too late.

I beat my wings.

A stray insect.

I ask for forgiveness.

It's not enough.

Tara's hand thrashes. Now it's enough: the sting of the slap, the red mark on my face.

The boys' delight. Their flashing eyes.

Tara cries.

I laugh. Straighten my back.

Her hand shakes.

She wishes she could hold me, kiss me. My restless child.

Once we've eaten everything is good again. The red has faded from my cheek. We clean our teeth. A boy carries a clay bowl of vinegar around and Maria hands out little scraps of fabric which we dip into the bowl. We rub it against our enamel. Our gums sting. It stings under our fingernails. We gnaw at our ragged cuticles. We laugh at each other, adjust our collars and dry our hands. Vinegar spills from the bowl and the sour smell tears at our noses. We take a pinch of salt from the tub and toss it over our shoulders.

I sneak a glance at the boy with the vinegar bowl. He sleeps in the purple room. He is slender. Long eyelashes. His hair like a dark helmet around his face. Timid. He moves with the grace of a kid goat, with swaying hips and narrow elbows, which sets him apart from the other boys and makes my insides sing. He looks like me and yet he doesn't. His moustache is downy and blonde, almost as invisible as mine. I wish I could reach out and touch it. I've seen the older boys kneel before the barrel full of rainwater and shave their faces with a knife, repeating the same motion: the blade flashes, a piece of soap in hand, they lather it up, shave. Red, glowing cheeks. This task at the barrel is an important one. But my moustache is light as dandelion seed. Like him, the boy with the vinegar bowl, who doesn't shave either, though he sleeps with the brothers from the purple room.

The boy rubs his finger across his lip. The muscles in his jaw course beneath his skin like blue strings. He looks up, meets my gaze.

In this house we have no names. But I know that a name is something you can give to someone, like a gift. Beetle. I call him Beetle. Shiny dark hair around his face. His movements erratic, his head twitchy. Like the beetles I've seen

53

in the forest, burrowing under fallen trees, hard smooth shields flashing in the sun.

I can feel it between my legs when he looks at me, deep in my thighs. I shiver, like I did when the boys poured icy water from the barrel down my back. My chest fills with air, pulls me so strongly to the sky that my vision goes black.

Tara lifts the bowl of vinegar out of the boy's hands and places it on the table again. We suck the salt dust from our fingers. Tara herds us together. Work, she says.

The younger boys crawl up the ladders, hang the big, fat garlands of garlic to dry. Now the garlic dangles above us in the door frames, swaying in the draught. I sniff the noxious air. Then the younger boys have to make the older boys' beds. Everything must be white and clean, like smooth, smooth marble. Is that understood? Tara commands. The boys giggle and pound the floors with their brooms, scrub the planks with marl and sprinkle them with fine, white sand from the sand closet in the attic.

I have the day off because I woke up early to help. And because Tara has forgotten everything again, the soot and the moustache.

The older boys walk in a line along the forest edge and gather twigs for kindling. They clamber up into the trees, hang from the branches, look back at the house. I'm in the kitchen, turning a paring knife in my hand as the blade beams, a narrow strip of sun, but soon the sun will disappear behind the trees again. The boys' white shirts shine in the forest dark, under the orange sky. The snow has begun to melt, the air is heavy and compact. In the darkening day I breathe down over the boys. They light a bonfire at the edge of the forest, the smoky smell invades the house, and the fire glows red long after they've left it. The boys weed the potato patch, they plant new garlic bulbs, they feed the hounds and the sheep in the red stable. I stand behind the door when they rush in, my heart beating heavily. The boys run past me. Laughing, sizzling, shouting: Fire! Tiny bonfires flare in their eyes, lick at their corneas.

I slip into Maria's room, into that endless night between the blankets and the blue shadows. I sit at the foot of her bed. Only a pinprick of light hangs above her pill bottles. Maria shifts in the bed, turns her back to me. A cloud of dust. She coughs. At rhythmic intervals she coughs up mucus mixed with blood. Her sheets are thick and dark with the sticky fluids that run from her mouth. I stack pillows behind her back, dry her lips. I lie beside her, breathe with her, hold her.

The mattress is so soft I sink into it, cradled between the shadows, the heavy metallic stench. The shutters are never opened. When Maria is at her worst, she can lie in bed for days on end, and I pull back her blanket to check if she's dead.

I bend down, unbeknown to Maria, and sniff her. The strange chemical smell comes from all the pills she swallows out of the little brown bottles on her bedside table. BAYER: HEROIN – EFFECTIVE AGAINST BRONCHITIS or

55

CARTER'S LITTLE LIVER PILLS or GELONIDA ANTI-NEURALGIA
– FOR FEVER AND COLD SYMPTOMS. These are the little
mantras Maria whispers as she opens them. I turn away
so I won't throw up, turn the bottles in my hands, lift the
lids. I fill my hands with the little white pills, sniff their
dusty, chemical smell.

These are Maria's tiny treasures.

Her room is a treasure chest.

I lick a pill. It burns bitterly against the roof of my
mouth.

Maria says: Everyone carries the catastrophe within.

I stroke Maria's hair.

Maria says: You're like a brother to me.

She takes hold of my hand.

I bring her a glass of blackcurrant juice.

Thank you, she says.

I put a damp cloth on her forehead.

She wheezes, gasps for air.

She says: I still can't imagine a grave.

Just a field.

A big, white field.

Wheat growing like white fur.

A sky like white roses.

She chuckles.

Maria regains some strength, drinks the juice I've brought
her, drinks it in little sips like a baby bird. I help her up out
of the bed. She wobbles and supports herself against the

wall. She pulls the curtain aside a little. I open the shutters and the fresh, cool air surges in.

She reaches out a hand.
Snow.
Melted snow.

Maria, do you think Franz Ferdinand will ever drive past our house?
Hmm. No. She laughs. She turns around and stares into my face. Strokes the hair back from my forehead. She tickles me.
I wriggle away.
No, I say.
Maria pinches my cheeks.
Little insect. Buzz, buzz, buzz.

Later in the day, Maria reads aloud to me from the newspapers lying open on her blanket. None of us boys in the house can decipher the letters, ants crawling across a white tablecloth. Tara brings the newspapers back from Budapest. They are Maria's most precious gift, apart from the pills. The crackling pages, the oily smell of ink. Of noise. I open them for her, spread them over the sheets like the wings of a bird. Maria says: Now the world has come to me. She reads everything, dark news stories, announcements and advertisements from Budapest, and not only Budapest but other parts of the world as well: Chicago, Helsinki, St Petersburg, all the places and all the cities I've never been to, all the names I never grow tired of hearing spoken aloud. I love to listen to her. The news, pulsating fragments of images that reach me in this house, through the silence, through the snow.

RICE HARVEST FAILS IN JAPAN

HARRIET QUIMBY FLIES ACROSS THE ENGLISH CHANNEL

MS *SELANDIA* LAUNCHED IN
COPENHAGEN BY BURMEISTER & WAIN

FRANZ FERDINAND GOES HUNTING WITH
THE GERMAN KAISER WILHELM II

WOMAN MURDERED, BODY LEFT IN SNOW

OSCAR FIEDLER. ZOOLOGIST. CONSERVER OF MAMMALS,
REPTILES AND BIRDS. TANNING AND TAXIDERMY

NEW OSRAM ELECTRIC LIGHT BULBS. IMPOSSIBLE TO BREAK.

LUNA THEATRE PRESENTS IN COLOUR: *THE ICE-COLD HAND*

I beg Maria for a single pill, and she relents. I imagine that the pill will cure me. That it will sink through my body and dissolve in my bones. That it will make my body clean and beautiful. That it will even everything out, make me clean on the inside, clean on the outside, make me look like the other boys, make me forget about Beetle. Beetle's swaying hips. Beetle's eyes and his long, soft lashes. The whir of joy and fear in my chest when he looks at me. Then I lie down at Maria's feet. My ears ring. The ceiling spins. I breathe in as deeply as I can, the walls and the windows bend inward, and I feel mighty. I'm in a little bell jar where I can hear everything and see everything, safe and happy, where no one can touch me, no one can do me any harm.

I am a night flyer. I live here between the house's walls. My cocoon hangs from the ceiling like a great, porous shadow. Soft, grey threads spun layer upon layer. I hold my arms close to my body and waver in the draught. The cocoon holds me captive. I'm stuck to the walls. I listen to the house and it tells me of my early years. Among the boys. A boy yet not a boy. Among the boys' elbows and teeth and laughter. The walls close in around me. The house's mouldy breath sedates me. Cradles me.

Tara sings:

> I *want a lock of your hair.*
> I *want a chunk of your cheek.*
> I *want a boy to call my own.*

In the dark, in the sweet, dizzying air of the oil lamp, in its violet light, I turn the knob and the wall grows, and the flame licks the glass. It is evening, and we are alone in the parlour. Tara is sitting on the sofa, her long, dark dress creased in folds over her belly. She's let the hounds in from the red stable, and they lie curled at her feet, sleeping. Their breathing moves their bellies and their shiny, grey skin.

Tara is carding wool, rhythmically rubbing the carders together.

In the spring, when sap rose in the trees and the night frosts were over, we pulled the wool off the sheep. Only after the frosts, otherwise they'd freeze to death. We herded the animals together, washed them gently in big, bubbly tubs of soap and soda. Shivering, wet creatures. Their cries were heartbreaking, and we consoled them like little children. Then we walked around the garden and waited for the wool to loosen so we could pluck it off in big, soft tufts.

I sit so close to Tara that I can hear her breathe in time with her zealous work, the breath flowing in and out of her lungs, the smell of her mouth: nicotine. Chemical tar.

The carders fill with grease. The smell of wool permeates the room, an odour of sheep fat and soil. Tara lets me touch the fuzzy fibres between the carders' teeth.

Then the hounds wake up and sniff me, snarl at me, climb to their feet. Their black gums hang in great folds from their open mouths. Their saliva drips. Come. They slink into the lantern light, their eyes shining at me. Tara is the only person they obey. The hounds are thin-legged and gaunt, and I'm afraid to run my fingers through their rough, grey coats. Only because Tara is here am I brave enough to get close to them. I lay a hand on their snouts, wet and cool.

Tara carefully rolls up the fine layer of wool in the lower carder and puts the fluffy bundles in a basket.

I help her spin the thread. The bobbin whirs.

Tara says: Were you the one who took the milk?

I bow my head, ball up my hands.

Refuse to admit it.

Never. Never. Never.

You know you can always get your milk from me.

Tara caresses my cheek, her fingers greasy from the wool. I press my thumb into a freckle on her cheek, and she grabs my wrist, holds it fast. I gasp in my tight shirt. I'm hungry. Tara pulls down her dress and I wrap my hands around her breasts, press hard at her collarbone and down to make the milk flow. Then I suck. Yellowish drops emerge from her breasts in stingy droplets. Her nipples are red and swollen, her breasts marbled. I lap up the milk greedily, though I'm thirteen years old and no one else in the house as old as me drinks Tara's milk.

The milk flows through my blood, makes me feel safe, drunken and dazed, like when I eat too many of the fermenting fruits that lie on the grass under the apple tree in the autumn, and which we gather in great sacks.

Listen.

Can you hear the river churning? Tara asks.

There's someone out there, crying.

A woman who gave away her child stands outside every night, washing its clothes in the river, Tara says.

Tara says: Such a repulsive poltergeist.

I feel a sob in my throat, like watery porridge that could suddenly push itself up through my neck, my mouth, overflow.

Who is my mother? I ask Tara.

Tara says: If my body could give birth, I would have birthed you. I am bound to you. Your mother came from Budapest. She came with you the first time, knocked on our door, but I said no. I unwrapped your swaddling cloth, and I said no. We'd never seen a child like you before. Then a day went by, and she came again. She laid you down on the steps and left. I opened the door, and there you were in the snow. Your face shone at me. Your eyes were so clear. You spoke to me through those eyes. I gathered you up. Opened myself. Leaned over you. I decided to raise you just like our other boys. I think you were left here at the house because we were meant to take care of you, me and Maria. We were glad to receive such a gift. The snow received you and offered you up again.

I lick Tara's face. Then I pry myself from her arms, run through the parlour, storm into the hallway, open the door to the garden and shove my hand down, fill it with snow, stuff my mouth with it, lap the snow up too. The snow is milk and I am a cat. I reach out into the dark garden, feel the tingling of the ice crystals, an inner joy at the sudden cold, and then a metallic shock rams into the roof of my mouth, the taste of soil and rust.

Hear my song of Our Red Mother. Tara bears motherhood in her like little black stones. She says I'm her only child. She says she's bound to me by an invisible ribbon. I think that I and my body are to blame for Tara's fury. I know my egg perplexes her. When I refuse to submit to Tara she gets angry. When rage flows through her, I call her Our Red Mother: Tara flies out of her skin and takes another form. A larger form. Our Red Mother rips a bottle from the cupboard, clutches it tight, presses it to her mouth, and the sweet brandy drips down into her eyes, bulging red from their sockets. Blood vessels take root in her eyeballs and make them big and miserable.

I call Tara Our Red Mother. I say it to myself, sing the name to empty her of rage. I feel her unease around me and I make it mine. A prickling in the soles of my feet, my hips unhinged. I feel dizzy, all the air is tugged out of me, and I collapse to the floor. Tara's voice grows louder and louder as she shakes me, saying that I've ruined everything, this house, this life. When Our Red Mother speaks to me, I'm ashamed that I was ever born and I want to curl up, drop like a sack of bones, rip the sheets from the clothes line. And at the same time I want her to take care of me, for I know that no one in the world can take care of me like she does.

I know that rumours are spreading about me. That the rumours seep out between the walls, out into the snow, and that the snow carries them down to the river, and the river cradles them and brings them all the way to Budapest. That the doctors and the scientists in the city have heard about me. That Tara talks about me when she drives off in her car. That they're expecting me. That they want to examine me. I've received a referral from the doctor. He wrote to a Dr Vajda in Budapest. Dr Vajda has an X-ray clinic, Tara tells me, he has the newest machines and the best education Zurich and London can offer. Soon they'll shine the lights through me, Tara says. We await my appointment.

BLEGDAM HOSPITAL
COPENHAGEN, 1952
(August)

Did you really drink her milk? Ella asks.

Oh yes, I lapped up every last drop! I latched on to Tara's breast as tightly as I could. The milk was sweet and putrid, fermented, it tickled my mouth.

Twelve strikes.

    And I slipped out of my skin like a blanched almond.

    And I glided into time.

    Suckled at the breasts that were offered.

    The breasts of the mothers.

    The milk flowed burning through my veins.

    At once newborn and ancient.

    A wandering soul.

    I knew everything and nothing.

    I licked my lips.

    My egg swelled.

    My yearning was the trembling cable of a grandfather clock.

A few days before I was born, Mother took the night boat to Aarhus. Ella was with her too. We sailed through the night, Mother says, eating sausages and liquorice in the big restaurant with its shiny tables and its chairs upholstered in dark leather. The boat rocked. Ella stumbled back and forth across the deck and Mother couldn't run fast enough to catch her. Mother waddled around, yelling. There was a snowstorm and flakes were driving down, sticking to the windowpane. They had to take distances with sonar. The boat sailed into the wind, and Mother and Ella got very seasick.

Mother said: And little you.

Mother said: You were angry, you turned and spun under my skin. Stretched my belly. First an arm, then a leg. I felt the first contractions on the boat. The pain was so deep and strange.

Mother says that, for many days after the birth, after they cut the pulsating, blue umbilical cord, disinfected it and tied it up, my belly button kept bleeding. A wound that wouldn't heal. Mother says that I just stared at her, angry, my hands in little fists, such a little creature with such great strength, and finally she had to look away. Who made you, you silly little creature, it certainly wasn't

71

me, she thought. She thought that I was a stranger, that I wasn't a part of her, but then the feeling passed and she cried, laid me to her breast, and I crept up and licked at the first sweet drops.

The hospital is airy and clean. Footsteps and voices blow through it. The building sits in the centre of the city, between wide boulevards, and it's as if all traffic and all movement is sucked in towards it, into these cool walls.

I lie here in the auditorium, unmoving, among all the other children, but we're much too far apart to talk to each other, silent in our iron lungs. I spin my threads in my shiny, glittering cocoon. We wait.

The nurses congregate in the courtyard. Their voices reach up to me and rise onward into the pink evening sky like long strings. I imagine them leaning against the wall, smoking cigarettes, unbuttoning the collars of their uniforms in the sharp air.

Ella whispers: Agnes, give me your hand, I have a surprise for you.

Ella smuggles in sweets in for me, and places them on my pillow. Althea sweets. I do my best to conceal my treasures from the nurses. When they turn their backs, I dig up my orange clumps of amber, full of little air bubbles, and greedily fill my mouth with the sweet taste of bergamot. Ella has another present for me, but only to borrow, she says, putting it in my hand. I feel it, a ring of steel thread and a fine, silky membrane. I can't guess what it is. She dangles it between her fingers, and says giddily: A diaphragm, it's a diaphragm. I blush with embarrassment.

Ella says: You don't even know how it works.
Ella whispers: You put it on when you're with a man.

I think about Ella and the men as a nurse dispenses my pills, which lie on a little tray, blue and yellow and white. The men stand over Ella. She spreads her legs, and their eyes flash as they fumble with the diaphragm, looking up at her hole, and they're all naked and blushing and bashful. My tongue is dry. The pills are just as enticing as Ella's sweets. The nurse lifts my head and gives me a glass of water with a straw in it. As she places the pills on my tongue one by one and I swallow them, my head grows heavy, metallic, her voice distant, and the room's shiny floors rise up towards me. The nurse puts hot compresses on my chest. She says: One day we'll practise breathing outside the machine.

She writes in my journal: *17 August, patient's respiration still weak, 22 days since admission.*

It's said that fruit and meat rot faster in the dog days, the month of August, the month we're in now. Ella reads to me from a book she borrowed from the library: Sirius approaches the sun, milk curdles, and dogs are prone to biting. In ancient Egypt, they celebrated the arrival of Sirius in the morning sky, believing that this was why the

Nile breached its banks, and why it grew warmer. Homer described Sirius as a bad omen, a bringer of unbearable pain.

There are rumours that the sickness sits in the blossoms of the apple trees. Children are forbidden from touching the flowers and eating the peel of apples. Schools and nurseries close, as do the train toilets, the paddling pools in public parks and gardens. Students are sent home and milk girls can no longer enter the hallways of the city's blocks of flats. They say the sickness is worst in the capital, but there are cases across the whole country.

The final stage of the sickness affects the functioning of the lungs. Breathing becomes lethargic, the brain and awareness grow foggy. Nerve synapses shut down. The whole nervous system degenerates, and sounds and smells become intolerable.

Agnes. My child. My mother leans over me, smiles, gently strokes my hair.

Mother. A sorrowful face. A face full of compassion. The smells of her citrusy perfume and her sunburned hands, glistening with Nivea cream. Her hands clenched in front of her. Far beyond her I can see the days in our house. The yellow terraced house on the outskirts. The house that always smells of charred meat and thick sauce, its curtains undulating in slow motion, waves between the green shadows of the garden and the glare of the mirror. I can smell the freshly mowed grass and the dusty, leathery scent of my books, and the cold tiles of the bathroom floor, bleach, peppermint and rubbing alcohol.

Mother is wearing her pleated yellow trousers. She clutches her leather shoulder bag tightly. Her skin is worn thin from soap. She doesn't belong at the hospital. She moves differently from the doctors and nurses, restlessly. Her hair billows, brushed up by the wind. Her cheeks shine with sun cream. She's holding an apple, she cups it in her hands, finds a knife, and cuts it into slices for me. She arranges them into a star on the plate and takes my hand. Her velvet hand inside the machine. Cold.

She watches the hands of the hospital clock, and we hear its ticking.

Like the tick-tock of my heart.

Her restless hands hold everything. Time, which runs. Fingers playing a tinny piano. The song of duty. She twists the handkerchief around her neck like she twists a head of lettuce before she puts it in a bowl, grates apples and celery, cuts figs into fine strips, presses a lemon, dissolves sugar in its juice. The house's shadows cling to her face. She never has enough time for her Agnes. Her Ella. She says: A mother must make money. Toil for her daily bread. There was a time when you drank my milk, when I held you in my arms, my warriors, but you drank and drank and grew away from me, drank till you were sated, dazed with my fat and my blood, sucked the very marrow out of me till there wasn't a drop of me left, just a loose husk of skin and hair, and I passed it on to you, all the rage and longing I had inside. She says: Look how you two have grown. She says: My work.

But now I'm sick. Now I'm lying in the iron lung like a little baby, like when I lay in the incubator. I call for Mother. Hiccup. Gasp for air.

Ella was always the taller one, the one who drank up the looks she got from the boys, from our mother. At her long, snakelike body, at her soft fringe falling over her eyebrows. Shining, sparkling eyes. Her beckoning shoulders, smooth and round as boiled eggs. It was never me but Ella who got little compliments, doting caresses, smiles.

Me: the slender, flat-chested one, my sharp nose inspiring no one's curiosity. I stood strong and straight, alone in the playground, playing hopscotch with rusty, bloodied knees, my head light as the clouds. I smashed my teacher's cup and swept the shards under the doormat, and it crunched so wonderfully when he stepped on it. I hid from my mother's hand afterwards. She gave me a slap, a glowing red spot for each finger, and she only served dinner to Ella that night – boiled potatoes with parsley and drumsticks bubbling with fat. Ella hid a drumstick for me, and under the darkness of my blanket I tore the meat from the bone, bite by bite. Mother gave Ella some curlers and she slept with them in her hair, propped up by pillows, wearing a bonnet, like a queen. The big, shiny curls made Ella even taller, drove the men even wilder. But now it's Ella who must step aside when Mother comes to visit. Mother walks quickly past her, sits by my side, and now it's my hand that lies folded within hers.

Who is my mother? I asked her once, and she shook her head at her silly child with all its silly notions, at my little head with its wavy hair smelling of cradle cap and sugar, at the things children conceive of, and, though it was obvious, she answered me as if I'd asked for a cookie or milk: I'm right here.

I ask: Mother, when can I come home?

Mother says: Soon. You're coming home soon.

Agnes. Look at me.

I close my eyes and say: No.

I'd rather keep my eyes closed when Mother is here, so she doesn't remind me of home.

Mother says: You're in good hands here.

Mother says: I'll get you a cookie.

I say: Over my dead body.

Mother says: Don't talk like that.

I say: I'll talk however I want.

Mother strokes my hands. You're a good girl.

Mother says: A girl shouldn't ask so many questions.

The porters lug great, white sacks of laundry down the halls, whistling as they go. A scent of green soap, vinegar and ammonia follows them. One of them turns to look for Ella, comes over to us. Ella plays chess with him, the tallest, thinnest one. They have a club, he and the other porters, and they play at night, he says, while the hospital sleeps. They light the boards with torches. They drink cognac. He digs a torch out of his pocket and clicks it on, lighting his face from below, grimacing. Then he shines the light into my eyes, but it's Ella he's looking at. He runs his hands over the wooden figures, moves his queen. Checkmate. His eyes are so clear, the irises almost white.

The other children's voices, bright and long as streamers:
    I can't sleep.
    I'm thirsty.
    I peed.

They call for the nurses, click their tongues, laugh up into the air: Miss Jakobsen, Miss Mortensen, Miss Frandsen.

Milky porridge in deep plates.
    Crying. Deep sobs.

I wish we could talk to each other. Physiotherapists stretch the children's limbs with one- and two-kilogram weights that hang from belts and strings around their hands and feet, to keep the muscles limber. The nurses give us juice, pushing their little carts with food, biscuits, porridge, rattling with blood pressure gauges and pillboxes.

I know what the other children wish for most of all, what they dream of: waffles with ice cream, a trip to the cinema, their little brothers and sisters dancing around them. What I wish for is a great big glass of thick milk. I wish for Ella's long body, her white socks and her ballet flats of thin leather. Her open lips. Her eyes, casting their spell, sparkling and beaming under her lashes.

The porter comes back, sneaks in like a cold wind. He stands beside us stiffly and gapes, shamelessly, not even bothering to feign some other purpose. His hands hang down, big and stupid and rough. Ella sits up straight, curls waving down her neck. I say a phrase I've heard my mother say: Look what the cat dragged in. We drive him away with our callous laughter.

When he's finally gone, Ella does my homework with me. The school year has already begun. The bells chime, students flock in. The playground is full, Ella says, but it's not the same without you. The playground is empty. The classroom is empty without your voice. I miss you, Ella says. I'm bored. Let's trade places. If only we could.

Because I want to know more and I can't go to school, I say: Read to me. And Ella reads to me. Physics and history are my favourite subjects, and Ella studies them with me, helps me with the hard words. We look up the ones we don't understand and write them down. She clutches the notebook in her hands.

We write: *Chronology (from the Greek χρόνος, chronos, 'time', and λόγος, logos, 'word, reason') is the science of measuring time. The god of time, Chronos, is the father of Chaos.*

We write a message to Mother: *Hi, time moves so slowly here. Have you forgotten all about us?*

When Ella is gone too, and I'm all alone, I watch the electric clock that hangs above the door. It moves its long, thin, insect legs. The clock is alive, trembling with every second. When Ella isn't here, I talk to the clock. I ask it about time. I ask it about the things it's seen. I ask it about the other patients. Who has been laughing, and who has been crying. I ask about the mothers. About the newborns, the skin of their eyelids, about their sour, white vomit. I ask the clock who it has abandoned here. Who has gone, and who remains behind.

My ancestral line: chronology marches on. I grow. Ella and I sit side by side on the sofa. A strip of sunlight falls in through the window and over us and turns our eyes transparent as glass. Mother aims the camera at us, yells: Smile.

I close my eyes. We're on holiday. It's a different August and I'm twelve years old. Mother has rented a little bungalow on the outskirts of an Austrian town. The soldiers at the border crossing stand at the ready with their machine guns, but when we get close to them they lower their sunglasses and smile. We follow the car's movements on the map. We make it to the Danube. We watch the dizzying churning of the river. We drink sweet, strong coffee at a little hostel on the riverside. An older woman waits on us, and we eat soft strudels while Mother drinks white wine and beer and chews her charred schnitzel and chips. We sit in the shade of a grapevine. The grapes are great, green tears.

We stop on the road on our bicycles, Ella and I, straddling them and looking uninterestedly at the camera Mother clutches in her hands. Then we ride away from her at a frenzied pace, leaving her behind, hurling ourselves forward with our fists clenched around the handlebars. We want to see who can get to the water first. We ride towards the river's quicksilver, faster and faster, as if we are possessed, whirled onward by an invisible force.

We lie our bicycles down on the riverbank. It's evening. The damp air swarms with mosquitoes and they stick to our faces. It's much too late to be out. We walk barefoot, the soil is alive with white larva. My T-shirt and long nylon shorts cling to my skin. I feel dizzy, and I know Mother will punish me when I get home. Ella vanishes into a thicket to pee, and when she comes back she has taken off her blouse. Her small, dark nipples are stiff. She is not afraid of the cold current, and she walks ahead of me, takes off the rest of her clothes, lets her body sink into the river. I follow her into the water. She dives down and I go after her. There is no sun, the water is a purple mirror now. We seek out the riverbed, like blind crayfish. Our hair sways above our heads, black shadows disappear in the algal depths. We explode, break the surface, sharp gusts of oxygen filling our lungs. We are only two flat silhouettes now. All our features have vanished. Then we lie in the sand, which clings to our backs, a coat of fur.

I tell Ella that I'm confused, that I don't know who I am. That I saw a strip of blood when I went to the bathroom, all that red filling the toilet's white bowl. That it comes once a month. Ella laughs. I can smell her body when she moves. Secret, salty. She gets back up, walks out into the water, takes a running start and dives, vanishing below the surface.

When we get home, I show Mother the blood. I turn my underwear inside out. The brown and rose-coloured stains in the cotton that I can't wash away. She buys me pads and Tampax. Soft, little tubes of cotton for me to press up between my thighs. I clutch the pack in my hand. I sit on the toilet and spread my legs. It feels dry and uncomfortable when I pull the tampon out again. Mother isn't shy, and she shows me how to do it. She's not ashamed like me.

Mother says: It's your time now. We should celebrate it. You're moving from one body into another.

THE SOUL FACTORY

(DICTIONARY)

The souls are transparent, like the night flyer's wings, like time. There isn't much space where they are, and they swarm inside a jam jar, flitting and fluttering against the glass like confused insects: soap bubbles at the membrane of time, trembling, bursting. Their hands are thin as spiderwebs. Child souls, gelatinous clumps floating in the glass. They cling together like larvae before briefly coming into sight above the fizzing surface.

Psychiatrists at the University of Virginia have been researching reincarnation for several years. Their investigations have been carefully documented. Employees in white lab coats admit children from the plush waiting rooms and lead them into the offices where the interviews are transcribed. When a child reaches a certain age, they may dream of other lives. Around the age of two or three, children often tell the researchers that this is not the first time they've been born. They recognize their ancestors' faces in old photographs. Some have birthmarks or scars that correspond with injuries to their body in another life. The children know that, no matter how much they explain to the researchers, they will always be wiser than them, will always know more than them.

TARA'S HOUSE, 1913
(illuminated)

I hold my breath. The mist is white. A powdery light pervading the forest through the tree trunks, its long, grey, porous fingers creeping towards the house. Winter's frost crystals are like flour in my eyes. The boys are ecstatic, running in and out of the trees, tearing off each other's coats, vanishing into the forest, into the mist. Distant, velvety shadows. I can hear their howls and loud voices, voices that coil around my bones and bite into my spine. I gasp for air in my tight corset, but should I ever dare to loosen the fabric of my shirt, wriggle out of my armour, Tara would be furious, would tighten her grip around my arm, spit and seethe and scream, and I would bow my head and sing, sing of Our Red Mother's rage.

I'm hiding behind the curtains. My breath is all I hear. Tara drives the car up to the house, enthroned inside that wild machine, surrounded by metal and dark-red varnish. The hounds stand guard around Tara's great metal apparatus. We boys are in awe of her as she tells us how it works. It's a Benz. We repeat the word, whisper it quietly as a spell. Tara is proud in the sweet-smelling leather seat. Straight and wild, her car shiny and brilliant. When she starts the car, the noise of the motor is louder than the churning river and the shouting boys. It sounds like a thousand little explosions under that iron lid. Then the great metal apparatus growls like the hounds. I take a step back when the car starts moving. Tara is going to drive me to Budapest, where I will be examined by Dr Vajda, she says. The boys shovel snow from the garden so Tara can get out. She fills the tank with petrol from veined leather canisters, lugs them out from the stables, fills the radiator with water. We await the motor's thousand explosions.

The boys are hares hopping between pink and blue shadows. They sing, their arms working frantically. They're just as excited, just as nervous as I am. They don't know anything about it, all they know is that Tara is going to drive me into Budapest. I feel sorry for them. I wish they could come with me. I wish they could leave the house like me. See what I see. But the boys stay here. The walls are silent. The house watches over them. The boys stand in a ring in the garden, turn their palms to the snow that falls from the sky. They take one another by the hand, walk towards the centre, then expand the circle again. They roll around on the ground, stuff their coats with wet snow.

Inside the house, Maria opens the windows wide. Tara pulls her coat on tight, the long, dark-blue woollen coat with red lining. She wears jewels around her neck, jewels she will take out once she leaves the house. They beam at me from beneath her coat. Amber eyes. Emerald eyes. Tara rattles the chains. She throws me kind words like bits of meat to the hounds, her hands sweeping through my hair, down my back. I follow her orders.

Tara says: Get ready.

Tara says: I'm proud of you.

She has an envelope in her hand. A printed card with the emblem of the doctor, the snake coiling itself around the rod of Asclepius. The time: 20 January, twelve o'clock. Be on time. Signed and stamped: *Dr Vajda's X-Ray Clinic, Budapest.*

I'm scared, I say.

Tara says: It won't hurt. I'll drive you there in the car, faster than the river flows. Tara rings her bell. The snow amplifies its sound. Blue lights whirl around me. Maria calls, and the boys run through the door. They stamp the snow off their heels, stamp the carpet dark and soft with their boots, stamping in unison. They come close. With their help, the sisters herd me into a corner. I buck in wild protest. The boys and the sisters shout as they tie a blindfold around my head. Tara rings the bell and the boys disappear.

I cry. I ask Tara: Why can't I see?

Tara says: No one may tempt you away from me. Not even the city.

At first all I hear is the crunching of the wheels on the gravel and the rhythm of the motor. Then Tara speeds up. We drive so fast. I didn't know such a speed was possible. I'm afraid we're going to destroy something with our speed. We drive faster than the fox runs through the forest, much faster than the hounds. We bound after time. Then the emptiness around me begins to move, pressing in against me like a great cloth, filling with sound. A girl's harsh singing. A harness creaking. The slamming of doors. Church bells. The river running. Animals. Hooves. Howls. A flood of sounds and smells. Sour milk. Sour urine. Hot tar and smoked meat. The sounds grow more powerful, louder, they enfold me entirely. Laughter, shards of glass, screams.

Dr Vajda. We're at Dr Vajda's office. When Tara loosens the blindfold, rays of light fall over me like rain. And then he's standing there before me. Tara withdraws, closes the door behind her. Now it's only Dr Vajda and me. He is tall and wears a brown lab coat buttoned all the way up. Little round spectacles. His pupils are enlarged behind the lenses, his irises dark green and as deep as Tara's jewels. He has a great, arching moustache. Long, slender hands that never rest: the nails white, long and clean, the fingers gripping his coat pockets. My heart beats so hard. He says: I'm Dr Vajda, so pleased you could come. Light breaks through the curtains and for a moment his eyes look transparent, like green water. He smiles. Dr Vajda has the light of the city in his eyes, in the folds of his lab coat, in his precise movements.

He sits down at his desk, and I stay standing. I straighten up, hold my head proudly above my stiff white collar. But the soft brown rugs are so deep that my boots sink into them like mud. Everywhere the sharp smell of disinfectant and new leather. Heavy, brown curtains and venetian blinds. Tall shelves of books, their spines red with gold embossment. White busts of men. Beakers and cut-glass bottles. On the desk is a long knife with an ivory handle, and instruments of various sizes gleam in a little glass cabinet. A great, angular chunk of amber, glowing like coal. Everything smells damp, sharp and shiny, as if the whole room were soaked in vinegar.

Dr Vajda asks: What's your name?

Boy, I say.

Tara calls me Boy.

He wrinkles his brow, takes off his glasses.

I'm not used to standing before strangers, and I try to inspire his compassion with the corners of my mouth, with my eyes, which I lower so he will treat me kindly. So he will help me.

Do you know why you're here today? Dr Vajda says.

Yes, I say. Yes.

You're going to light me up.

Dr Vajda nods for the first time.

Dr Vajda says: I think you're a clever little one.

I say: I don't want to make Tara angry.

I say: I just want to look like the other boys in the house.

He says: The rays will tell us everything.

About my egg? I ask.

Dr Vajda laughs a short little laugh and pulls on soft white gloves.

Everything turns towards me. My face haunts the window-panes, trapped in the wavy surface bursting with air bubbles. I step closer, press my ear to the glass. The city whispers to me. Footsteps and voices rise and fall. The river churns somewhere below, spray from the brown waters rising to the glass. I feel like a hundred eyes are watching me. Great, dark chestnut trees press against the panes, fogged by my breath. But maybe the city isn't there at all. Maybe I'm the only one in the world now. Me and Dr Vajda.

I run my fingers over dark mahogany furniture, over beakers I can barely discern in the darkness. Wires and rubber cables dangle from the ceiling. A machine with two enormous coils of wire, apparatuses like strange sewing machines I can't understand. I put my hand on the cool metal and it crackles, a heavy electric jolt. The pain is dizzying, nauseating.

We know the power of progress. The power of science. I step closer to Dr Vajda. You've come to the right place, he says. I begin to unbutton my shirt, the collar scratching my throat, and I'm about to take off my shirt when he raises his hand: Keep your clothes on.

Dr Vajda leads me across the floor. I lie, fully clothed, on a plate of metal held up by four wooden legs. He covers my body with a sheet and presses me down on the plate. He says that the rays can't be seen with the human eye, that it doesn't hurt. He says the rays can travel through doors and fabric, through flesh and bone. He takes hold of my wrist, clutches my hand. Don't be scared, he says. But I am scared, so scared that I want Tara to come in and take me away, that I want her to drive me as fast as the wind back to the house in the forest. I toss and turn while he waits for me to calm down. Everything vanishes from under me. I sweat. He takes a step back and hides behind a tall screen, where he can watch me through a porthole. He counts down. Now, he says. I don't know what he means, because nothing happens. He switches on the electricity. Then come the rays.

Dr Vajda calls them X-rays. Roentgen rays. X means unknown. They call it the new anatomy of light. Tara is proud, she stands tall when he shows her in. She drapes her dark coat over the back of a chair, as if she were at home, takes a little cigar from her case and offers one to Dr Vajda. The delicious smoke curls around our heads, drapes the apparatuses with a blue veil. The three of us sit down. A feeling of momentousness thickens the air like Maria's mint jam. Dr Vajda coughs and his dark-green eyes water. Light flashes in Tara's jewellery, which rattles ominously as she leans forward and says: We're worried. We don't know how things will work out. She combs her fingers through my hair, adjusts my shirt. We think you can help us.

Dr Vajda wrinkles his brow again. Yes, he says, but we must be patient.

Dr Vajda says: We can't see the rays, but they see everything. They can read the human body.

He shows us the pictures of my body, revealed by the rays. They sit up on a board like a row of witnesses, illuminated by a lamp. I stand still, the floor spins. Everything is heavy and light at once. My skin is stripped away, my veins are shrivelled, and a gauzy veil lies between my bones and the world.

The pictures show the deepest part of my body. Everything human has been peeled off. I don't know what's left. It is night, and the light is a light that belongs to the night. Or a very bright day, much too bright, mountain sun. But the rays shine through me. My blood has stiffened and crumbled. Dr Vajda says it's a picture of my pelvis. I turn the pictures over again and again beneath the lamp, ponder my dark, diffuse flesh. As if my gaze could finish developing them.

Everything I know about my body is gone: my nails, my veins, my blood and flesh and skin. My hip floats on the glass. My skin is dissolved, wiped away like soap. The world has become transparent. I tremble. Because it's me, really me. Because it's true. It is my body, my tailbone, pelvis and cartilage, Dr Vajda says, my wing-shaped hip bones. My body, growing in its strange, irregular form, like a withered flower that persists in its blooming.

I feel dizzy, feverish.

What is it inside me that shines so brightly through my bones?

Dr Vajda says: Before a person turns fifteen, the sex cannot be determined by the skeleton. But in adults, differences between men and women are visible, particularly in the skull and the pelvis.

He says: We must keep a close eye on you.

Your beautiful pelvis.

Tara nods and they shake hands, strike a bargain in which I am the goods.

Dr Vajda says that he will print the pictures in a scientific journal, to share their findings about me, my body, the walking mystery that I am.

The great, jagged words of Dr Vajda drift through my head, and I don't know what to do with them. My eyes flicker. Why do I feel so hot? I'm dizzy. Maybe I really do have a fever, or maybe I drank too much of Tara's milk before we left the house. The milk rises in my throat.

Dr Vajda tells Tara that they shouldn't be stingy with me, shouldn't keep me hidden away in the house, because, he says, everything belongs to science, and Tara nods, holds out her rough, cracked palms, says she understands that she was mistaken, that they should never have kept me from the outside world, that this should have happened long ago, that I'm no longer a secret kept from the world, for everything must come to light, nothing shall be hidden.

I ask: What's wrong with me? Am I sick?

Dr Vajda says: There's nothing wrong with you. You are just as God made you.

I ask: How did God make me?

Dr Vajda says: As an uncut diamond.

Dr Vajda strokes my chin and says: There's nothing to hide any more. We don't want you to change. We're very pleased with you, and we want you to remain as you are.

I walk over to Dr Vajda and take his hand and whisper: Does this mean I can show myself to the boys? Tara gets embarrassed and swings her hand at my cheek: No, no, never. In the house you are Boy. Her slap is so hard it wipes away the room like a heavy rain, and I fall to the floor and stay there until Dr Vajda wakes me with an ammonia-soaked cloth under my nose.

A mirror hangs in the hallway of Dr Vajda's clinic. Its shiny surface moves like water. My face follows me. I hold a hand up to the glass, and when I move it, it vanishes as quickly as it appeared. I puff up my cheeks and blow out so the mirror fogs. I look at my dark eyebrows, which have grown together between my eyes, which have become darker and denser, and I glide my finger across my forehead, down my sharp nose, turn and circle each of my cheeks. Tara says that it's dangerous to look at your reflection, that the mirror will steal your soul. She says that if the mirror breaks then your soul, too, will break, and you have to gather all the shards and cast them into the river, which will carry them away and wash them clean again. Then your soul will disappear from the water and be born in a new body. At the house we have only the water barrel in which to see our reflection. Water can never break, but it can't show us our true faces either. I stand there until Tara appears behind me. She ties the blindfold around my head, takes my hand in hers, squeezes. She says: Come.

BLEGDAM HOSPITAL
COPENHAGEN, 1952
(September)

In September we listen to the song of the ambulance's sirens.
  Blue September.

The mirror above the machine catches my face, pale, defiant. And it shows me the whole sickroom, with its shiny tools and linoleum floors, stretchers rolling by in the hallway. The mirror shows me my skin, reveals every detail in the sharp light, crowned by the eyebrows arching across my forehead. The nurses have cut my hair short so it won't get tangled in the machine: a sharp fringe, cropped above my ears. I lift my left hand to touch my face. My eyes are deep, gleaming lakes. I look into them, into the glossy vortex of my pupils, the marble rings of my irises, and I see the other. I see Dr Vajda's office, its soft rugs, a face appearing in the mirror. A stench of ether and sweat. And for an instant: those big, wide eyes. I stare into the mirror. We're separated by a thin membrane that glows dimly like the inside of a mussel shell. I can't move, but you lean forward, your lips parched, your minute movements shaky, as if in slow motion, your face distant, cool, and yet so close that we breathe in time. Sparkles and beams beneath your eyelashes. A flash from me to you, into the glass and back. It is us. My body feels so tender, I tremble. How can it be that we are two and one at the same time? I watch you. I reach out my hand, but I can't touch you. My fingernails glide over the cold glass. We have the same hair. Our big eyes open wide.

The hospital walls close in around us. A quarantine has been instituted. The hawthorn hedge around the building has grown higher, its shiny leaves arching to the walls, guarding us. Visitations are prohibited to stop the contagion, so I have to make do without Ella. The days stand still. Great, white plains of time. Parents have found boxes to stand on outside the window, and we see their heads bobbing there, necks craned in the hope of catching a glimpse of us. The nurses shoo them off.

They say the sickness is still spreading. The television's scratchy broadcasts report on the epidemic, and ambulance drivers fill the room with stretchers. There are beds out in the hallways now, because there's no more space. Sulking faces, little moons turned to the ceiling.

The whole city is quiet, holding its breath. The only sounds are the sirens, all day and all night. The waiting rooms are so full that they've put up tents on the lawn. The air is heavy with rain. The lane leading up to the hospital is muddy. Ambulances arrive, stretcher after stretcher. Here they come. Death's hotel. The final station. Child souls.

Only the press are allowed inside the hospital. The doctors show foreign journalists around, let them photograph us. Their cameras flash at me. Nowhere in the world is the epidemic as dire as here. The journalists are different from the nurses and the doctors, from the mothers and the fathers who come to see their children. They smell of smoke and whisky. They wear dark blazers with the sleeves pushed up. The women wear woollen skirts and curls in their hair and they smell like permanent solution and lilies. They laugh a lot. They hold their shiny pens like weapons. They gather around me, their curious eyes shining, their cameras whirring, and I am blinded by the lights.

> *Are you Agnes?*
> *Do you miss your old life?*
> *How does it feel to breathe?*

The doctor translates their English, and I answer as best I can. They praise my courage, showing me their white teeth and clean hands. Later, one of the journalists sends a newspaper clipping of the article she wrote. I hardly recognize myself. I'm smiling at the reporter, and my face, lying on its tray with the rubber collar around my neck, seems to shine as bright as the iron lung itself. I beam like a little defiant sun.

White night. I listen to the sounds of the iron lung: its creaking and rattling and singing. The sighing of its ventilators and pipes. At night the porters flit about with their torches, up and down the hallways. The ventilators emit a constant scent of ammonia. The nurses on watch whisper. The machine hisses. The pump pumps. The machine sucks electricity from a great battery on the floor. It drinks and drinks. At night I miss Ella. I call her name in my sleep. I dream she's lying beside me, and when I awake the sheets are wet and smell of her sweat.

I call for a nurse, lift my left hand to caress the cool, rounded wall of the iron lung, knock three times, and wait for an answer.

The machine's rhythm is steady. Air pumps in and the big membrane fills like the pouch of a giant frog. The sounds of a great, grinding apparatus. The machine keeps going by itself, without my help, but it doesn't start until I'm inside it. The shiny, green surface of the cylindrical tank reflects the sun's rays as the nurses draw the curtains.

The iron lung rules over me. It choreographs my movements, manages the flexibility and elasticity of my muscles, my breath. It decides when I will move and when

I will be still. The only thing that's mine is my voice, like the tones of a powerful pipe, and the air that's pulled through my lungs, that inflates my tissues and makes them collapse again. And when I surrender to the mechanics of the machine, when all my muscles relax and it moves my body, the iron lung plays me like an instrument and blows its song through me.

Agnes?

How are you feeling today?

We're just going to turn you over and change your shirt.

The nurses powder me in great clouds of talcum. New patients go by in the hallways. Stretcher after stretcher. I hear the sounds of laughter out on Blegdamsgade, the rush of the cars, the soft, September wind slipping through the window, the ivy that climbs the walls rustling its dry, purple leaves. The nurses laugh. Their pens and syringes rattle as they take turns bending down to kiss me. They have a special fondness for me, they say, because I've been here so long, because I've surrendered, do not resist. Because I am no longer afraid.

The scent of camphor, the scent of vinegar.

The hospital's wings are far apart, so disease can't spread between them. Each building protects its patients. I can hear children outside, playing over in Amor Park, their bristly voices filling the street. Vapours of newly mowed grass, a ball's rhythmic bouncing. The figures on the statue at the park's entrance cling to one another: Athena shielding her children from the arrows of the goddess of pestilence. I stretch the fingers of my left hand. Milky light. Evening comes in through the trees.

I look at my hand, at the contours of my skin, and it dissolves as I start to cry, because the pain is too much. As if I really am disappearing.

A team of cleaners comes to wash the machines. They come at lunchtime, when the nurses are out. They come like a choir thundering down the hall, shouting and singing and scrubbing. They hold their brooms high like flags, then they lean in the doorways to look at us, at the iron lungs arranged in rows. They walk among the machines, lift the hatches and pinch us for fun, and they sing and spit and knock their buckets and slosh noisy soap across the machines, they wash drops of blood from the floor.

They sing the song of the stork:

> O *little frog, I'm taking you,*
> *quack-quack, quack-quack, quack-quack.*
> *My three hungry children are waiting for you,*
> *quack-quack, quack-quack, quack-quack.*

Agnes.

Look at me.

One of the men bends over me, stares at my face in the mirror.

He sits in the chair where Ella usually sits and starts talking to me. I feel cold when he says my name. I don't want to answer him, so I tighten my lips, clench my hand.

The other voices vanish, and all I can hear are his hoarse words. He speaks of eels, the eels he catches in a lake outside the city. Oh, eels big and fat as a girl's thigh, he says. I go out in the evening, when it's about to get dark, and I set out my rods in the water, and you can see their shadows under the surface, and when the eel bell rings and an eel starts tugging, I pick up the rod and tug it back. I'm at war with myself, he says, clenching his fists. The eels he has caught are writhing on the bank, bloodied, coiled around his ankles. One of the eels has a tail split in two, a tail divided into two long, dark and slimy fingers which dash from side to side, an eel that looks like the others but isn't one of them. This eel stares at him with wild eyes, vicious, and all its rage fills its rasping and hectic writhing, its two tails thrashing on the ground, a rattlesnake attacking, a weapon, a dance of death.

The cleaner opens one of the hatches and reaches in. His hand is restless inside the machine. Heavy. His pupils widen as his big hand moves across my shoulder, seeks my breasts, moulds itself around them until I scream, scream inside and hope Ella can hear me. But she's not here. She doesn't answer.

After the cleaner's hands, I no longer want the nurses to touch me. Now I scream inside when they open the hatches, and they mumble soothing words and I see their bewildered faces hanging in the mirror above me. And I know they write it all down in my journal, they write of my recalcitrance and my anger.

Agnes, my little mouse.
  Agnes in the iron lung.
  Are you sleeping?
  Ella calls to me.
  She puts her hands over my eyes.
  Guess who? She giggles.

Ella, it really is Ella. I'm so relieved when she bends over
me and I see her face instead of the man's in the mirror
over the iron lung. The quarantine is over, for now. Visitors stream in and the nurses fight back their tears. Ella
kisses me. Can she see any change? I don't tell her about
the hands that reached through the hatch, the hands inside
the machine.
  Now Ella banishes his face.
  Him.
  The cleaner.
  O little frog, now I'm taking you.
  She wipes the mirror clean.

I can only speak when Ella is here. To the nurses I respond
in one-syllable words, I mumble and spit. But as soon as
she is here again, I become soft and gentle. I suck up my
juice through a straw, hold her hand. When she kisses me

on the cheek, it's like I'm floating, and I briefly forget that I can't walk.

Sister of my heart.

Ella.

Will you always be my sister, no matter what I do? No matter what I tell you?

When we were younger, Ella fell and scraped her knee. She cried, and I bent down and sucked the blood, the sweet drops seeping through her skin's small pores. The blood was generous, it rose and it flowed, and I sucked and sucked until the wound was dry. Her blood tasted good, like iron and soil and salty skin, and I held my mouth to her knee and didn't let go.

I watch Ella eat her packed lunch, thick slices of bread with butter and ham, her lips glistening with oil. I witness her transformation. Her face has changed in the short time since I was admitted. She has pierced ears and pimples, oily skin, and her breath smells different, like onions and mayonnaise. Her voice is deeper when she bends down to whisper the sweet and hopeful words that only we two hear.

We don't fight like before, like sisters tend to fight. Not in the hallway between our rooms, not under the sheet we've stretched out like a sail at sea, between shadow and sun. Ella listens to me now, and I make her promise that what I tell her will stay between us, and none of the world's men will take our secret away from us.

Ella whispers.

Agnes?

Agnes?

Have you ever been so close to someone it made you dizzy?

Someone you like.

Heart pounding.

Pulse racing.

So close you could just die?

TARA'S HOUSE, 1913

(the purple room)

The grandfather clock in the parlour beats like my pulse, *tikketikketik*.

Counting the evening's hours.

I flit around the oil lamp in the kitchen.

My shadow is orange in the light.

My nails are orange.

I tremble.

I click my tongue. I want to kiss someone.

Like Tara and Maria kiss us every night before we fall asleep.

Like the hounds lick our feet with their great, rough tongues.

I lap up the milk until the whole pitcher is empty.

An ember springs from the fireplace and singes my skin.

A mouse scurries over my foot.

My little fist clenches in my pocket.

I stole a fountain pen from Dr Vajda. It's glowing in my pocket, burning through the fabric.

A marble shaft with a golden tip.

My little treasure.

My bones seemed to shine through the fabric.

The words he wrote down.

The pelvic bowl.

The secret of the sex.

With this pen he whispered those words.

He gave me a contract.

I signed.

A cross.

A cross for science.

Sealed my fate with the ink that flowed from the pen and stained my hand.

Tara wrote her name.

There we are, she said.

We'll write to you with the time of the next appointment, he said.

Very good, Tara said.

We'll be expecting you, he said.

Yes, Tara said.

Yes, I said.

I hear Tara behind me.

Boy, she calls out.

Little Milk Moustache.

I wipe the milk from my lips with my sleeve.

With her hand on my shoulder, she said: Come.

She's not angry about the milk.

She says: Now it's your turn.

It's your time now.

The door to the purple room where the older boys sleep is locked. Tara has the key, she turns it. I've only been here a few times. We step inside. I've heard the boys' screams so often that they resound through my head. Nervousness sits in my skin, a shining membrane. I stand still, smell the scent of paraffin wax. Goosebumps, quick shivers.

The walls are purple, the window frames pitch black and gleaming. There is no sunlight here, and it is no place for tears. The boys sit on their beds, they've taken off their shirts. Their eyes are as big as two-korona coins. A single lamp is lit. Their naked skin shines at me, their slender muscles tense as they tighten their fists, and hairs rise around their tender, swollen nipples.

The white geese that the boys watch over are clumped together in a corner. They puff themselves up. Their feathers look unnaturally glossy against the purple wall, as if coated with varnish. The boys pluck their feathers when they're bored. Then they line up and blow the feathers across the floor to see who can blow the farthest. The geese sleep with the boys. They honk under the blankets, which move like ghosts. The geese lift their wings, their yellow beaks, hiss at me. The boys pick up the birds and put them in their laps, stroke their feathers until the geese calm down.

The faces rusty contours.
 A forehead in the darkness.
 Beetle. Shiny dark hair.
 Look at me.
 Beetle, the shy one. Much too shy.
 Beetle, the beautiful.
 Beetle is just as tall as me.
 We're alike, Beetle.
 You and I.
 Our bones shine.
 Our bones are eternal.

I take another step into the room.

So close to you I could die.

Each boy has his own bed. The iron frames line the walls. They are also painted purple, and beneath the beds are coarse, woven straw mats, which the boys spit on. There is a bench under the window where I could sit. But I don't sit. I hold all my possessions in my arms, my summer jacket and my winter coat, my shirts, my brown leather boots, a bar of soap and a sewing needle, which Tara gives us so we can patch our own clothes.

Tara was the one who made the decision: Now I'm going to show you where you're to sleep. With Tara, I've turned my back on my old life, the yellow room and the little boys, their snot and tears. Now I can't wait any longer. I'm already taller than the youngest boys' noses, taller than the crowns of their heads. My voice has sunk into my throat and sounds deeper now, like when Maria knocks on the zinc pipes because they're clogged with leaves. I must abide by the house's order. My boy, Tara says, because in this house I'm still Boy, though the rays have shone through me and offered no proof. Dim shadows press in around me. I feel tense. The boys from the purple room drum their fingers against the wall.

The smell of garlic is heavier here, sharper, sour. It saturates the walls. Portraits of the sisters hang in gilded frames, and a stuffed marten with no eyes dangles from the ceiling, spinning in the draught from an open window.

Tara points at the great mahogany wardrobe. This is where the boys get dressed, she says.

I nod. The wardrobe is big and dark and covered with thin, shiny sheets of metal, so no one can drill a hole through it to see inside. This is where you, too, will change your clothes every evening, Tara says, and I nod.

I turn back to Tara and give her a sign: I'm ready. You can go now. Let me stay here.

Where will I sleep? I say out into the room.

The boys rise lazily from their beds, tugging their shadows with them. They crouch around me in a circle, breathe in my face. One of the boys, the tallest, offers me his hand. Sootmouth, I whisper, because though his hair is as light as sun-bleached hay, he has the darkest moustache by far. Sootmouth, I whisper, you're the one I fear most. Sootmouth is as thin as the slenderest birch trees in the forest, though he eats gluttonously: pickled apples, pörkölt and great, steaming bowls of stew. He's the one the other boys obey, he need only wiggle the tip of his little finger. Cold, light-blue eyes. His Adam's apple dancing below his tight lips.

He says: Who says you get a bed?

He says: You've got to earn a bed.

The geese honk and flap across the floor. The boys rock back and forth on their feet. I drop my things on the floor. Now the boys are right up close and they prod my shoulders, test me. I pull back. They quickly check my hair for lice, run a fine-tooth comb through it. They turn over my hands to see if my nails are clean. Then they inspect all my belongings, as if they want to keep them separate.

Each boy has his own hook. That's where I'm to hang my jacket, and I am to leave my boots below.

Beetle. He crouches with the others, looks at me, and I ask him without reserve: Where do you sleep? Beetle points to his bed, and I say, I'll sleep here, here in the bed beside yours, and I pull back the quilt, though I know the bed belongs to someone else. I lie on the bed, smell the sheets, stiff and yellowish like flaps of old skin, an odour of soot and oil and sweat rising from the mattress. I will make this bed my own. The boy who sleeps in it stares on, his pupils contracted, purple as the walls. The geese honk behind me, and I raise my head, return his stare. All eyes are aimed at me.

Sootmouth says: You must choose one of the geese. You must choose your opponent.

Sootmouth says: Get on with it.

They're testing me, and I know what it all means, what the boys want. And I have no choice but to obey. I must show them that I'm as strong as they are. I stand up and take a step forward, and, as if they know what's about to happen, the geese beat their wings frantically. The boys have risen too, they draw closer, clap in unison. Bile rises in my throat. I look over at Beetle, his squinting eyes. Don't be afraid. I look into the blue flame of the lamp, draw courage from it. I choose a goose, the smallest. Its little black eyes blink, blink, the lids strike like lightning. With my fingers around its neck, I twist, and its wings beat out, and there's so much strength in the animal as its body presses against my chest that I nearly fall over. I wring its neck, its long, serpentine neck. The bird strikes back, and control flows between us, from the bird to me, muscles and veins taut, and I scream, a low scream through tightened lips, until at last the animal goes limp, its wings droop, and the boys cheer as the life drains out of it. My trophy. Bliss sits just beneath my skin, like a knife.

Later, when the day is gone and evening swims in the purple of the walls, of the floors, I gather my nightclothes and lock the wardrobe from the inside. My feet are clammy, sticky on the cold metal. The darkness falls so fast around me. I peel off my trousers first. My pulse rises. I hear the boys giggling. Beetle is right on the other side, and I try to distinguish his voice from the others. *Give me back my blanket. I wish you were dead.* Be light. Unbothered. A kid goat. I pull my nightshirt over my head. Button it up. I lean my cheek against the door, open it a crack and watch him, watch him through the darkness. When I'm done, the boys are already lying in their beds, their stiff bodies outstretched, hands over the covers, as Tara insists. I crawl into my bed. The fabric is so cold, it clings to my skin like wet leaves.

I drift into the night-time hours. We tick on into the purple darkness.

The boys' breaths saw at the night.

I turn over in bed.

Beetle is awake like me, his breath heavy.

I shiver.

Fear and joy braid into one.

I want to tickle him with my little swells.

I stroke my finger across the skin above my lips, feel my soft moustache growing.

I feel the glands growing beneath my skin.

My hand moves down over my belly.

My curved sex.

My egg.

I show it.

Tempt.

I sleep until mid-morning. The sun spins in the sky, far away from us. The goose spins from the ceiling where the boys have hung it, and bile rises again. Purple shadows flow through the room. The boys sit cross-legged on the floor, great needles in their hands. The boys have plucked the goose. It spins from the ceiling, with its bumpy, pink skin and yellow beak. Its strangely naked neck, once so proud, is limp. There is no trace of blood. The white feathers lie in a pile. The boys are sewing a pillowcase out of soft, white fabric, their needles drawing great arches through the air. They stuff the feathers into the pillow. They hand it to me ceremoniously: This is for you.

I feel the milk-white fabric, the feathers so light inside it. The fabric glides through my fingers like silk, a silent rejoicing. I feel light. Now it's all mine, the purple room. And Beetle, too, is mine, with all his wonders, his warm body and his dishevelled hair, and the sighs at night from his bed are mine.

I put on my grey woollen coat and my winter boots and step out into the garden. A light longing flows through my body. Orange light glows within me, beams from my skin, my nails. As if I've swallowed a whole bottle of Maria's pills, a whole bottle of Tara's schnapps. The air above the snow is blue, and a shiny husk of frost clings to the branches. Laughter bubbles up in me, from my diaphragm into my throat. I'm full of something new. Little Milk Moustache, Boy from the purple room. Boy. That word is my permission. That word is the only thing that counts in this house. The boys are my brothers. In our white shirts tight as corsets we're the same children, we're alike. In the house I fit the mould: we eat and clean our teeth with the same mechanical motions, we carry our faces like polished coins, we button our stiff collars. But my tongue tastes of rust. My tongue wants to taste Beetle's skin, to lick salt and vinegar from his fingers, and in this house boys are not to kiss. Awake in the darkness, I saw Beetle's eyes shine as he leaned over me without a word, his breath blowing down on me, making my nipples stiffen. All thoughts of flesh and skin are forbidden in this house. We're not supposed to stare into each other's eyes. Maybe I'm sick like Maria. I long for her pills.

My coat is open, the fur tickles my neck. I sweat. My feet are weightless as I lift them through the snow. Tara has let out the hounds. They play together, roll in the snow, throw themselves on top of one another, panting, biting. They run along the edge of the forest and disappear among the tree trunks, into the blue darkness. Then they come back again, circle me.

Maria has shown me how to throw little stones at the hounds to still them. I take a step forward, they growl restlessly, bunch together. They come closer, press their noses to my groin. Usually I kick them back, push them away, but today I've stolen dates and hazelnuts from the kitchen, and I hold out my hand, lure them. The hounds sniff my fingers, skim my skin with their cool, damp snouts. They take a few steps behind me, whine, bare their teeth, but I am firm. I hold out my hand, throw the nuts in front of me, and they follow me to the edge of the yard. I step into the shadows with the hounds right behind me. The soil yields with a sucking sound. We're in the forest.

I feel Tara's breath on my neck, and I turn around.

But there's no one behind me.

It wouldn't be so strange if Tara's breath were still clinging to me like cold, sticky glue, for this is the first time I've been over the border.

The invisible border between the forest and the house.

Here and no farther, Tara says.

So I can still see you.

So I can still hear you.

So you're still my boy.

This is Tara's decree.

But now my belly is bubbling with urges, and now I have the hounds with me, and the forest lures me in, the snow's white blanket, the cold fragrance of moss and pine needles.

It's so strange. Nothing happens. When I start out, I'm afraid the birds and the branches on the trees will turn grey, turn to stone and tumble down on me like an avalanche, as Tara has said they would if I were ever to leave the house. That the forest would yawn open with its white, living roots, its mouldy soil and its wet breath, and swallow me whole. But the forest is still. It stretches before me, waits for me.

The hounds' eyes are grey and shining. One of them is panting. They scramble over the ground, unaccustomed to this much freedom, muscles straining under taut skin. They nudge my arm with their snouts. The smell of their excrement is intense, rotten, and I bury it beneath the snow. I whisper to the hounds, and they obey.

The forest grows denser. The snow is heavy, deeper. I sink in and the white substance rises to my knees. The green moss takes hold of my heart, grows around it, makes it soft, and I lean my head back, gaze up through the wispy treetops and laugh. The branches sway. I lie in the snow, stretch my body. The snow's impression of my body stiffens into ice. Shadows become visible, green and blue. Flutter up like birds. The hounds lie flat, studying me, almost entirely still. The light behind them is red. Breath blows from their nostrils, their stomachs rise and fall. There is a strong smell of shit and saliva and bacteria. I stand up and look into the forest. I see paths in the snow, made by animals or people. They meander, disappear between the trees. I want to follow them, to walk and walk, never turn back. Great drops of sap roll down the tree trunks. The trees cry and sweat.

I call the hounds, and they run to me. I turn around, mimic their movements, tense my muscles, curve my back, race over the cold, wet leaves and steep drifts of snow. I run so fast that my body rises from the forest floor. I leap over creeks and fallen trees. In the forest my body is light, my arms and legs light.

Once I'm deep in the forest, so deep I can't see the house or hear the boys any more, I pull down my trousers. I crouch down to pee, and it tickles as the transparent little drops speckle my boots. The hounds dart around me, lick the yellow liquid from the soles. They are quiet. They don't bark. They don't growl.

The hounds brush my hands with their snouts, rub themselves against me. I put my hands on their stomachs, feel them like bellows, seek them magnetically, absorb their warmth into my hands. I press my ear against their fur. With the hounds, I am myself. No longer am I under Tara's control, between those stone walls. No longer under the burning marks of her slaps, her shame-on-yous. My whole body buzzes. I go down to the river and the hounds follow.

The water is cold, frozen to ice.

I lie on the bank. The ice on the river creaks.

Several eels lie in the snow, gleaming. They've been pulled from the river through a little round hole in the ice. Everything moves in their still-living bodies, little spasms like electric shocks, open mouths. I feel them, their scales clinging to my fingers like grains of salt.

I put my hand into the hole, and below it I see a great, red pool, rising, spreading. It's the eels' blood, sloshing below the ice. The deepest red I've ever seen.

The pool grows before my eyes.

The pool swirls under the glassy sheets of ice.

The red comes from the city. That's what Maria says.

Everything that is forbidden, that we mustn't see, Maria says.

Maria says: Red is the colour of the city. Red curtains and red lining and red silk underwear. Organs flayed open. Wine-red urine.

The river flows past the house, it flows past Budapest. The river tells me of the city and the world, but in a way that's different from Maria's newspapers. The river has seen other countries, Maria says, its water flows across borders like wind, down through Europe. The ice lights up in the red winter sun, and red runs under the ice. The water sings of flesh and skin.

My hand is cold and blue in the water. I pull it back, spread my fingers. I possess powers unknown. I open my trousers, rest my hand atop my curved egg, its tender, soft skin, I feel it pulse. Something in me transforms, like a great pit full of blood that grows and grows. I rub the folds of the egg, carefully at first, then harder, and I forget Tara, and it's as if my body comes loose, in new movements, seeking. I feel it grow between my fingers, all my blood rushing in to fill it, tender, painful. I throw myself down into the deep snow, lick my hand. The red flows through my brain, my dazed and trembling body.

I sing along with the river.

> I want a lock of your hair.
> I want a chunk of your cheek.
> I want a boy to call my own.

When I get back to the house I hide from Tara, and here between the stone walls I tremble, pink, tender and steaming like a boiled piglet. I wash my fingers with soda, rub them together until they're blue and raw. Tara finds me in the hearth, covered in soot.

Here. Tara.

Our Red Mother.

Raging.

She tugs me out by my ear, burning hot, pulls so hard she tears my earlobe, and I scream.

She says: Where have you been, Boy?

What have you done?

I took a walk by the river.

Nothing else?

Nothing else?

No. No. No.

You must always tell me where you're going.
You may never take the hounds with you.
Never.

After she's administered her blows, stinging red, and I've quaked beneath them like the boiled piglet I am, her hand grows still, and I ask: Where does the river flow?

She says that the river flows all the way to the Black Sea. At the end of the river is the sea and behind the sea is the sky, the same sky you can see here.

I say: I want to follow the river. The river is in me. Do you understand?

The light is green on the snow, green like Maria's sweet peppermint water. The fattest flies wriggle on the cream's surface, tugging at the skin. I am in the cellar to quench my thirst with milk. Knowing it will send Tara into a rage. Knowing she will offer me her own breast. But I don't want to drink her milk any longer.

Then the flies grow still, floating on the surface with their wings outstretched. I push the butter churn across the floor and put it up against the wall, pull myself up, and balance on the barrel so I can reach the highest shelves. I steal one of Tara's bottles of schnapps, which are hidden behind the cream and milk bottles. I clutch the bottle tightly and the golden liquid glugs inside it. No one sees me. The house tells me with its silent walls that I am allowed to take it.

I lure the boys into the forest the same way I lured the hounds. They're sitting on their beds in the purple room, legs dangling. The geese honk about their feet and peck at the floor. Purple shadows cling to their skin. Beetle and Sootmouth are among them. The boys file their long nails. The boys whistle, sew the tears in their coats with a needle, pass the thread around. Sootmouth pricks his thumb with the needle and three dark-red drops spring forth. He sucks up the blood. The boys look up when I come in. I

134

show them the bottle. Hurry. Don't be afraid. Their grins glisten, they pick at the pimples on their cheeks. They hop down from their beds, pull on their boots. We shut the geese in and creep down the hallway. The sisters are slumbering, lying dead in their beds. We sneak past their heavy afternoon nap. I shake the bottle, hold out my hand, you see, it's so easy. Coats on, quickly, crack open the door.

The house spews us out over the threshold. No one, there is no one who can hear us. I've bought my way up to the highest spot among the boys. I feel holy. My mouth tastes like soil. We go past the water barrel. The water is dead, metallic, a lid of ice blue and dark green. The house looms behind us.

We walk in a row, solemn, our necks stiff, stepping in each other's footprints until we cross the forest edge. It's good to be in here among the tree trunks. Here we can smell the soil and touch the bark. The trunks are statues, dark purple with the damp of twilight. The iron-green pillows of moss shine. We walk over the ground, the bulging veins of the trees, a damp, orange crack of light. We follow each other. We take turns leading the way. We can no longer see the house. The forest wraps itself around us.

The bottle glugs and lures.
I sing along.

> *I want a lock of your hair.*
> *I want a chunk of your cheek.*
> *I want a boy to call my own.*

I graze Beetle's hand with the cold glass.

 I am open, erect.

 Nearly bursting.

 Ready to be plucked.

 My eyes beam.

 My hair is shining.

 I preen, mighty.

 Take big brave steps.

 The bottle casts its curse.

 I know it.

 Today I am the most beautiful of all the boys.

Our bodies come closer together, in the half-dark we draw close to one another, spiderwebs hang above our heads, hanging on tight like wigs. My nerves shine through me.

 Then we sit down, we are a circle. I can feel the snow melt and wet my clothes. Their faces are expectant, smooth. I look up at the whirling treetops. It's as if everything is here, between us, among the trunks. The schnapps tickles our mouths. We take turns drinking, pass the bottle around, drink as if it's the thickest, loveliest milk. We feel the sharp liquid corrode our throats, slosh in our stomachs, until it prickles in our fingertips, turns out the lights, makes our brains dizzy. We share cigarettes, knowing we have to be careful, whispering that the sisters mustn't see the smoke rising, mustn't hear us. The smoke is sharp, tears our mucous membranes. The air is a red veil between the trunks. A pheasant flaps low to the ground. We fall to the forest floor, stand up, and let ourselves fall down again.

The bottle glugs.

The bottle gives me power.

I sing the bottle's song.

It says: Follow me.

The boys say: Pass the bottle.

The boys say: You're one of us.

The bottle spins between us, it twirls in the middle of our ring.

The one the bottle points to.

The bottle sings. Around and around.

The one the bottle points to is the first to be kissed, I say.

The others laugh.

No.

No.

No girls here.

They giggle.

Red-cheeked, the schnapps burning.

Sweet plums, plum schnapps.

The green glass of the bottle.

I say: We're in the forest.

Tara isn't here.

She can't see us, and we can't see the house.

We're not in the house.

We can do what we want.

I'm whirling, and the bottle spins, past Beetle, points to one of the other boys.

Sootmouth. Sootmouth with the cold eyes.

He sits with crossed arms.

He looks down at the ground.

I stand up.

I walk through the ring.

Lay a hand on Sootmouth's shoulder.

He stares back scornfully.

The circle is breathless, expectant.

I want to turn around, but I bend towards him.

I open my mouth slightly, and he opens his. He has eaten sour cabbage, and the acid exudes from his warm lips. I search for his tongue, which wraps itself around mine like a slug, and, since neither of us know how it's done, saliva fills his mouth and makes it big and soft and slimy. It feels so disgusting that we both spit on the ground.

He jumps up. No, he says.

No.

The others sit in silence, disgusted.

And my chest doesn't lift me to the sky like when Beetle looks at me.

Beetle in the circle.

The green glass deceived us.

It was you I wanted to kiss.

You.

We stand up.

Beetle's eyes rest on me.

His hands hang down, childlike, big black half-moons under his nails.

And the tall Sootmouth looks at us, and he sees us looking at each other.

He spits again.

It drips from his chin.

His eyes flash.
I spit too, knees shaking.
I say: Follow me.

I feel light. My brothers, we scratch secret signs and messages in the bark with our long nails. We draw big wide eyes that stare back at us. We write our initials: B... B... B. In the twilight we walk to the river, onto the ice. We spread our arms. We skate across the smooth surface, polish it with our soles. In some places the ice is thin and our feet go through it. The slushy ice crunches and sucks. The trees bow over the river, their leaves yellow coins under the ice. We lie on our stomachs and look down through the layers of brittle glass. We writhe like metallic eels. We knock, and the ice quivers. It creaks and cracks in narrow fissures. We look up and breathe in. I turn around. Beetle's eyes float in the half-dark, find me among the others. The whites of his eyes shine yellow. I meet his eyes. We glide into each other.

The boys skate over the ice, light and graceful, arms outstretched. Then their voices grow distant. But Beetle is right beside me. You can't go now. Beetle smells warm and tangy like cardamom, sharp with the bright milk that flows from the boys' dangling flesh. I can't hear the other boys any more. Now there is only silence, for us to fill, for us to drop coins down into. The snow's blue shadows come out to hunt. Beetle's freshly ironed clothes rustle, the word *home*, which Maria has embroidered with new rose-coloured thread, gleams. He shifts his weight from one foot to the other. He reaches out for me.

I see him against the bright snow, stretching his body like a soft, bendy membrane. He breathes down on me, breathes cigarettes and onions. He takes hold of my wrist with one hand, with the other he strokes my chest, and I stiffen, shake myself loose. A heat pounds up through my body, makes me dizzy and confused.

We stand on the riverbank. Just the two of us. The bottle is empty. I sling it out onto the ice and it spins wildly around itself. *Ssh, ssh.* Come here. Snow sprinkles from the branches, grains of silver in the air. Gently, Beetle opens my coat and my shirt, and I let him do it, lean forward. The cold immediately spreads over my throat and my chest, turns my skin blue, bumpy. It's me, me and Beetle, and his big lips and shiny hair and his hands so hot and open against me that his fingertips singe my skin. Beetle is panting under the layers of fabric. His hand under my shirt, he caresses the small, round swells. Curious, exploring, gliding. Then I push him back. We look at each other, stunned, flushed. I quickly pull on my shirt again, button the collar, fumble with the small black buttons. Beetle runs in circles elatedly, sucked into the shadows and shoved back out again. I look up through the branches, watch little spots of purple light flow over the treetops. We are weightless. We are held up by the clear frosty air. Soon the light will disappear completely. Behind me, I hear Beetle laugh.

BLEGDAM HOSPITAL
COPENHAGEN, 1952
(September)

Who are you, you who have made your mark on me? Dark, pageboy hair, your eyebrows grown together like my eyebrows are growing now, fat, bushy slugs across your forehead. You stand at the forest edge outside Tara's house, a fan of screaming green light, quivering like a fawn. The green is also in your eyes. I want to be closer to you. Your smooth pageboy hair and your sharp nose, the dark strands of hair that cling to your cheek. I blow at your fringe, and your hair stirs gently. I reach out a hand. Long strands of pain. Your skin clings gently to mine. You move into me. Night flyer. Don't be scared. You lie inside me like a child, cradled behind my skin like a little babushka doll.

Is that you?

Ella is staring at my lungs, which hang on the wall above the machine. An X-ray. There is the inside of my body, so shiny and true. The two dark sacs of my lungs hang in the slender cage of my ribs, and the fat snakes of my spine wind up through my throat. She can't tear herself away, she's been standing like that for a long time, across from the photograph, as if it were her own shadow, as if the photograph were clinging to her. The lungs, bronchioles, the big arteries and veins, the wings of my shoulder blades. Inside, blood rushes silently, like a river, but you can't see that.

Ella is wearing sunglasses and a necklace of imitation turquoise. She doesn't take off her sunglasses. She can't keep anything secret any longer. I was out last night. All night. With a man, he invited me out. The night was long. We drank beer at a bar. I had my necklace on, this one with the turquoise stones. It's strange, when I think of it, how the light was so strong and unnatural, yellowish, turquoise like the necklace. He smelled of fish and peppermints. Mother doesn't know, of course. Mother must never find out. We walked through the streets of the closed city. We stood in an archway. He told me to take off my clothes, and I wanted to do it quickly, but he said slowly, slowly, and I didn't understand why. He sucked on my breasts, he examined every part of my body, as if I were the sick one, Ella says, laughing. And we both laugh. But when Ella looks away, I cry in the iron lung, because I know I'm about to lose her.

I say: You are my sister of the night. You are my sister of the day.

I say: Don't go.

I say: You're the only one I can trust.

Ella shakes her head. Then she takes my hand. I'm right here.

The collar around my throat is softer than flesh, and it tickles. When I'm alone again, I touch the inside of the iron lung with my left hand, so smooth and cold. I rub my palm against its cool belly. I think of Ella at night, Ella with the man, naked in the archway, the cold air slipping like a bed sheet around their skin. Shoulders shining in the darkness. When I scratch my nails hard enough on the wall of the iron lung, threads of pain run down my spine. My left hand over my thighs, between my legs. The little rift, so soft. The membranes unfurl themselves under my fingertips. The iron lung moves with me, humming its low electric buzz. My blood boils. The iron lung changes temperature too. The sheets of metal, layer upon layer, a current of heat glowing around me. My body opens inside the closed shell. I summon all my strength into my left hand. Fumbling, rubbing, pressing, I am new and whirring, and a shiver runs through me, lifts my whole body so miraculously over the sheets, my mouth and eyes open wide.

Ella and I. We were born at opposite ends of the year, with only thirteen months between us. I was born when the light starts its advance, Ella on the darkest day of the year. But now we've switched it around: I go deeper and deeper into the night, Ella carries the light with her.

In school I always sat in the back row with the boys. So defiant. Anger was a flame in my breast. I was overflowing with questions that the teachers never had time to answer. They turned their backs to me and sighed. They said a girl shouldn't ask so many questions. They said a girl should behave, be quiet, sit still. They didn't want to waste their time on me. They would send me out of class and I'd go out into the playground, lean my head back and look up into the mild sky, the catkins of the birch trees stroking my cheeks. I'd watch the mothers waiting for their children when school finished, in their ironed grey woollen skirts. Their nervous, tired movements. Shiny hair. No one breathed. Their metallic nails and red-painted lips that pressed kisses down upon the children's heads.

History class. The teacher picked up a piece of chalk: Agnes, sit down. He talked and talked, so fervently that the chalk broke, that the blackboard shrieked, and he laughed. Time has a direction, he said, and he drew it there before us. He turned his back to us, his shirt blotched with big sweat stains that looked like giant maps, as he arranged the events of history along a curve that rose across the blackboard. He wrote the years on the board, the important ones, the ones we needed to remember: 1914, Franz Ferdinand's blood in Sarajevo, his blood on his uniform, Austria–Hungary falling apart, Europe crackling, the first great war, then the famine, the thirties, the horrible years, the war that followed the war, the atom bomb, which was thrown down on Japanese cities, and now onwards, progress, a great unbroken plane of time.

I gave up on asking. I dropped my questions into the dusty air. I spent long afternoons in the school library instead. I read everything. Geography, history, physics, chemistry, anatomy. I read about the expanse of the globe and the body, about the conjoining of bones and cells beneath the skin, about lung tissue and arteries.

I conducted my own experiments. I collected jellyfish in a bucket on the beach and put them into bubbling tanks. The salty water evaporated and settled into a slimy film on the panes, while the tiny eyes around the edges of the jellyfish stared at me through the glass. The other children gaped at the shrivelled, foetal, transparent beings, *Aurelia aurita*, that I displayed in the hallway outside the classroom.

Who was I?

I read about the atom bomb, about the incredible shape of the mushroom cloud, about the orange explosion, as if sunrise and sunset were happening at once, a fireball covered with glowing masses of dust, about the force that flings bones and skin and hair up into the air, that destroys bodies so easily, as if they were made of thin paper. About the deadly dust that falls and rests on the ground. I read, and it was as if the cloud, the dust and the colours rose from the pages of the book. But it was never enough. I always wanted to know more, more than what was in the books, more than the teachers knew, and more than I myself knew.

I wrote my name with dark-red, greasy fingers on the teacher's desk. Fingers greasy from the pastries I'd eaten, red from the blood between my legs.

Agnes.

Agnes is my name.

The history teacher says:

Joan of Arc was thirteen years old when she started hearing voices.

The Virgin of Orléans.

There was war in Europe.

The Hundred Years War had lasted ninety years.

She bathed in the Loire, great and shining.

She cut her hair so she could wear a helmet.

She led a whole army.

Wore men's clothing and armour.

Had two small swells beneath her blouse.

Was stubborn.

Defiant.

On the pyre Joan let her clothing fall off.

The Cardinal said: You said you were following God's command when you put on men's clothing, with nothing to show that you were a woman.

She was naked before everyone so they could see who she truly was, that she was a woman, before the flames licked her flesh.

Can I lick your tits? one of the boys from class asked me as I was standing at the mirror in the lavatory. I knew my face so well in that mirror, between the spots of rust. My sharp nose stuck out from my face, which milked the light from the tiles. I straightened up. My breasts rose in the centre of the mirror. Small and round. I massaged them with a soft hand under my blouse, they swelled, ruffled my blouse. I drank a glass of thick milk, licked my fingers clean, my cheeks licked red with anger, with shame.

Come on, can I? he pestered me.

I answered: Over my dead body.

The teacher looked at his clock. The bell chimed for the end of class. It was noon. A wild ringing. We sprang up. Grabbed our lunchboxes and ran out to the playground. Light and pollen dripped from the birch trees. Wax papers were fluttering birds in the shadows.

The girls skipped and sang.

Do you want to know
what the little boys do?
They beat their drums,
they beat their drums, bum, bum!
Do you want to know,
what the little girls do?
They dress their dollies,
they dress their dollies, like this!

When we came back in from the playground, when everyone had taken their places again, I stood up in front of
the teacher. I walked over to the blackboard, spat on it
and wiped it clean, so the curve disappeared and I turned
white and sticky from the spit and chalk dust. I turned
to see the history teacher's face, which was wide with
surprise, alarm. I let the glass of milk float, then shatter
across the floor. And now I will say: History is a river,
great and shining. We bathe in it. We are born in it, again
and again we rise from the water. Now I will say: We are
no longer in the time of school chalk. Not day after day in
single file. Not in the time of progress. We know nothing
any longer, everything is broken, everything is only shards
of glass we can't put together again.

The nurses push in the television. The screen is aswirl. Images flicker, powdery, blurry, they flow through my brain like a thick grey porridge.

The TV studio is full of smooth surfaces. Shiny pots and polished knives. The white, soft uniforms of the chefs, who move like sleepwalkers among their tools: eggs are whipped into peaks with sugar and milk. They teach the viewers how a sticky pie is put together using buttercream, sprinkled with raw, painted coffee beans, and how you divide the crust in two using a thread and a knife.

The announcer lady's voice turns serious, then comes the news, an interview with a politician in a heavy suit and square glasses. He brushes a speck of dust from his shoulder.

He says: We are in a new time, a time born with new threats.

He says: Two Swedish planes have been shot down by Soviet fighter jets over the Baltic Sea.

The Soviet Union, he says.

The threat from the East. It's getting closer.

A clip from Churchill's speech in Fulton, Missouri, 1946: *From Stettin in the Baltic to Trieste in the Adriatic, an iron curtain has descended across the continent. Behind that line lie all the capitals of the ancient states of Central and Eastern Europe. Warsaw, Berlin, Prague, Vienna, Budapest...*

The iron lung peels away great flaps of my skin. It hurts so much. My skin grows into the sheets, grows together with the fabric. The bedsores spread, red and brown scabs forming all over me, and the physiotherapist with the strong, tattooed arms turns me every morning and every evening so the sores won't spread any further.

The machine works with my body, compresses my chest and makes it expand again. It does its work so well that the doctors beam with pride and caress the iron lung as it empties me of spit and fluids. My breasts grow smaller, vanish back into their hollows, and the machine milks my blood, the blood that flows so thick under the moon and which Mother says makes me a woman. Now it has stopped.

A nurse changes my shirt. She finds a new one in the porter's pile and stretches out the fabric between her hands, looking back and forth between me and the shirt. The shirt hangs between her hands, a size smaller than the old one, a ghost crisp with starch and detergent. She says that my muscles have atrophied, that lying down for so long has made my body shrink. The nurse pulls the new shirt over me, and it is so rustling and clean that I shiver. It has the hospital's scent, which has also become my own – of great, bright rooms, of bleach, of soap flakes and baking soda.

Last night I had a vivid dream. I woke from the dream out of breath and confused. In the dream, my skin had melted into the machine. My skin was as thin as marbled wax paper, but so strong it could be stretched over the whole machine like a nearly transparent membrane. It was as if the skin belonged to me but was no longer wholly mine. I couldn't be pushed out of the iron lung. I couldn't leave it. Beneath the skin were my organs, creaking like unoiled machinery. I laughed, but it was impossible to say whether it was me laughing or the iron lung.

THE MACHINE

(DICTIONARY)

The machine and the skin flow into each other. The surface is a shiny, polished mirror. It is a symbiosis: at times the human has control over the machine, at times the machine has control of the human. My lung muscles are manipulated by the machine, which unfurls around my body like grey ashen wings stiffened into a frozen, shining form. Inside the machine, time moves very fast and almost stands still at once. It splinters into long, thin threads and connects my body to other bodies that once lived.

First developed by two Harvard professors and put into production by the industrialist Warren E. Collins, the iron lungs are produced at a factory outside Boston. The mechanics walk across the field in the cold, frozen morning and clock in, rubbing their chests to keep warm, their work clothes dark and stiffened with oil and tar. Recently, production rates have gone up. Their strained muscles must work faster and faster. The engineers come by to inspect the work, to wipe the surfaces of the machines with rags soaked in petrol. Rows of iron lungs gleam in the factory. The factory produces death machines that keep children alive for a time, but time is fleeting, it seeps out slowly through the cracks and defects in the machine, like the last breaths of oxygen. A bitter cold: time is only borrowed.

TARA'S HOUSE, 1913

(euphoria)

Pictures of the city, splintered and shining like shards of glass, pour through my night.

I crouch on the floor and sift through the newspapers Maria stacks in great heaps outside her door. She saves every one. *Pester Lloyd, Népszava, Neues Budapester Abendblatt.* I pull them out of the pile, one by one, dog-ear the pages. The oldest papers crinkle drily, yellow and stiff, and the faces stare at me blindly. Maria points at the letters, says *rib bones* and *corduroy*, she says *factory-made.* The words Maria pronounces when she reads from the newspapers make me so happy, they are words we never hear in the house. I whisper them to myself. I memorize them. But I'm not sure if the words belong to me or if they're just random, if they've lost their way inside this strange head.

Between the sensational headlines and shiny photographs, I search for something that has to do with me. Photographs of men at cafes, looking into the camera, squinting in the sun, with moustaches and dark hats. Women in great dresses, long necklaces, with serious expressions and drooping cheeks. I bask in the big city's sun. Crown myself with the men's hats and the women's jewellery. I can step into the picture and pull their faces down over mine, become the dancer standing on tiptoe. The body in the photograph shines in the tight, smooth clothes, the hair smoothed back, the arms stretched high above the head, the muscles and tendons almost painfully taut. Tiny breasts are visible beneath the thin fabric, round swells. The costume is nearly transparent, it could be a man or a woman. The dancer is wearing a mask. A mask of leather so you can't see the true face. The mask is so tight it seems melded to the dancer's skin. My tongue waters, I feel hungry. The heavy scent of the ink intoxicates me, its oils rub off on my hands. I'm so dizzy that my vision blurs and the letters stick to my corneas.

Yes, he's lovely, isn't he? says Maria. She bends over me and I can smell her tarry breath. Her fingers slide searchingly across the photograph. A famous dancer. His body is no human body. Imagine that. It isn't made of flesh and bone, of blood and fat like ours. He is lighter, he can jump higher, be carried on the air like a bird. A prodigy. Vaslav Nijinsky. A body made by the gods. He dances, and no one can dance like him.

Maria becomes cheerful as she speaks, her red cheeks soft as damp soil. She is rejuvenated. She shows me how to bend and stretch my arms, she pinches my sides when I fall. And I keep falling and get back up. I keep going, I don't give up.

Up on your toes.

Maria takes hold of my hips, leads me across the floor. Stretches my arms out.

Like this.

She caresses the two little swells on my chest, cups her hands around them, says: Little apples.

Ssh. I bat her hands away.

I get away with my insolence.

I want to be the dancer.

I lick the soot from the kitchen tiles. Rub a line above my lip. Draw a thin moustache. Like I did the time Tara got angry.

Her red slap ringing.

I am not afraid.

To twirl around myself.

Bold.

To be the dancer.

Look under skirts.

Bathe in spotlights.

Sing and hum.

Beat my wings.

So light today.

And there is Beetle.

As if out of the blue.

In the parlour.

And Maria has disappeared.

The snow gleams.

The boys are out.

Beetle, I call.

He sees me.

His shiny, dark hair.

He is standing right in front of me.

Hello, he says.

I stand tall, filled with desire from the city's pictures. My eyes shine with their reflection, with stolen sun. My skin is soft, little burn marks from the stove glow in my palms. My steps grow lighter, I am floating slightly off the floor. Take what you want. Sweat breaks out on my forehead, dew in my palms. I stretch out, take his hands, guide them to my hips like Maria did. Beetle, come here. Beetle doesn't resist, lets them lie there. So big and soft like clay warmed by the sun. We face each other, we are the same height. I blink, stroke an index finger across his cheek. I have fastened strings to his loose skin with great hooks and I lift it like dough, and his arms and legs move along with mine. I am the fisherman, the puppeteer: I've got you, now you can't get away.

We glide across the floor.
    Like Maria taught me.
    Around and around.
    Delirious.
    Hands on each other's hips.
    Two short steps, three short steps.
    There is air beneath us.
    Wafting like the curtains.
    Clumsy calves.
    My blood boils.

Everything capsizes, everything explodes. From inside and out. Eardrums, pupils. My egg pulsates, swells, turned towards him. Garlands of garlic twirl in the draught. The furniture of stained oak and mahogany are dark animals, the clear winter light shines. The grandfather clock chimes. We grow together there in the parlour, become more than ourselves, more than our outlines and shadows and voices, our flesh, which overflows and melts like butter. We hide in the fireplace. Beetle stretches himself towards me, presses himself against me. I open my mouth slightly and his tongue parts my lips, winds between my teeth, cautious, soft. I kiss him back, and it feels different from Sootmouth's kiss, my pulse pounds in every nerve ending, his tongue tastes sweet and smoky, like tobacco, his face is smooth and tight, his lips open.

We throw a party for ourselves and take out the finest coloured glasses, the ones we drink out of at Christmas and Easter. We hang them from the ceiling so the sun's rays race through them and a beaming carpet of light falls onto us in yellow and green and blue.

We are four eyes in the parlour.

Flashes and rays under our lashes.

Flashes from you to me.

Flashes from me to you.

We find a piece of coal and draw a fine, thin moustache above Beetle's lip, which quivers as I draw.

He kisses me again, the fat dance of his tongue below the roof of my mouth.

Boy, Beetle calls, whistling quietly. He licks off my moustache. Licks up the soot.

We laugh again.

An echo of each other.

We hiccup laughter.

Our lungs burst.

We take each other's hands.

We feel fortunate, like when Tara is in a good mood.

We find Tara's necklaces, the most forbidden thing we can think of, in the bottom of a chest of drawers in her bedroom. They rattle round our necks. Amber eyes watch us.

Now we can also be the women of the house.

The women of Budapest.

Their veils and smiles and laughter.

They are waiting for us.

If we walk through the forest, I say.

If we walk all the way through the forest, we will come to Budapest.

There is soft corduroy and mirrors everywhere, I say.

And men and women with big hats smile at us.

They wink at us.

They drink strong Turkish coffee.

They say: Come here.

They say: Sit down.

And they all smoke cigars like Tara, I say.

We sit down, I say.

And we sit there in the sun, I say.

And we smile back at them, I say.

And we also smile at each other.

The sun shines in our glasses.

We laugh.

And we are no longer the same people we were in the house, I say.

Now we've left behind the people we were in the house.

We are free.

Beetle says: No.

No.

Beetle says: The butchers have buckets of blood that they empty into the river, and people lie on their stomachs and lap up the water and roll around on the ground like barrels and talk nonsense like drunkards.

Beetle says: That's what Tara said.

The water turns red.

Do you believe that?

Maybe.

We laugh.

Then a door is pushed open.

Then someone rushes into the parlour, a dark movement.

Wait, be quiet.

My hand on Beetle's shoulder.

Discovered, we've been discovered. Dizzy with joy. Dizzy with fear. And everything vanishes up the chimney, an endless inhalation of soot and ash.

Then we laugh, because it's only the hounds.

They've come up from the milk cellar with their snouts big and white and their tongues hanging loose, smacking at their mouths.

At first the creatures are silent, then they see us and bound towards us. Clumsy, much too big for the little room. We laugh with relief, tug at their loose, black gums, kiss each other, kiss the hounds, wet and happy.

In the evening, when mist rises from the trees, we herd the sheep into the stable, Beetle and I. The sharp fumes of warm animals fill the air. We muck out and rake up new hay for them, we gather in our arms the soft, cottony wool that falls from their skin, we straddle the railings and mimic their sounds. Grunting, rasping. The sheep look at us with their glassy eyes. We laugh when we crouch down and they blow on our necks. We nudge them, rest our ears on their bellies, press our cheeks against their indigo udders as they chew and tear the hay with their teeth, and juice runs down on our hands. We lie every which way in the hay, pull straw from each other's hair. We open our shirts and let the sheepbreath billow softly over us, and I think to myself that this is a wondrous time, and I breathe freely in my loosened shirt, my ribcage billowing wildly up and down like the waves in the water barrel when there is a storm and the wind blows over it.

It is the last day of January.

You've grown, Tara says.

I walk taller, straighter than before.

I balance on the bed frame.

Preen atop my bed.

The other boys laugh.

I show them the dancer's enticing pose.

My eyebrows grow dark across my forehead.

I am light with Beetle's kiss.

I spread my wings.

I am a bursting membrane. A blue soap bubble over Maria's sink.

The soft skin above my lips.

Everything belongs to him.

I grow heedless.

I show Beetle the fountain pen. Dr Vajda's fountain pen, my finest treasure. He turns it in his hand. Its gold tip catches the light. Beetle folds his fingers around it. He makes himself hard and smooth as an apricot seed.

Who gave it to you?

It was a gift, a gift I got.

From who?

I can't tell you.

Tell me.

No.

Then give it to me, says Beetle.

He sighs in contempt.

He presses the point against his palm, and it draws a big, dark spot on his skin.

Beetle takes hold of the pen with both hands, uses all his might, and it cracks.

I scream.

No.

I am summoned to more consultations. Some with Dr Vajda, others at Semmelweis University. I don't tell Beetle. I leave the boys. Light streams from my bones. I leave the house. It is my and Tara's secret. Tara drives the car, the motor churns and explodes. A blindfold around my head. The tree trunks in the forest count themselves as we speed by, I can feel them through the soft fabric that covers my eyes. My body feels light without the weight of my bones. It's strange how easy it is to forget the boys. How easy it is to forget Beetle. Now it's like the fine and shining thing between Beetle and me is gliding away on the wind. Even Beetle's soft tongue, even Beetle's long kiss. I long to feel chosen. I feel like a precious stone in the soft seat. I want to make Tara proud, I want to be her Boy, her Dear Darling. As soon as I touch the car's soft upholstery, I am sucked into the darkness, into the speed. The rumbling of wagons, the screams of women, the clack-clack-clack of hooves in melted snow. We stop abruptly. I crawl onto Tara's lap. She says: It is your duty. I nod. I can no longer say no, the examination has already been set in motion. I hold her hand and squeeze it. I am a little, shiny gold coin, the most valuable one they have. I know Tara wants the best for me, that they all want the best for me.

The assistants guide me down a long hallway in the university's Institute for Anatomy. The day blinds me when the assistants loosen my blindfold. They're wearing long white smocks. They greet me without touching me, put their arms to their chests and bow slightly. I lean back my head and look up at the high ceiling. Everyone here speaks softly. The sombre assistants brush my hair, tie it up, and give me sugar cubes to suck on because I'm dizzy. The sugar surges through my body like Tara's schnapps. My footsteps echo through the corridor. Sounds become bigger here. I know I'm the one, the one everyone is waiting for, and I pull their gazes after me like white threads. The assistants open the door to the auditorium and show me the way. There is a heavy and sharp smell of rotting wood, of anise and chlorophyll. A skull as tall as a person is drawn in chalk on the blackboard behind me. The jaw gapes, parted into a smile.

The high ceiling and dark mahogany furniture overwhelm me, the seats soar above me. The professor is serious, he gives me his hand. He rings a shiny bell. We can hear the students in the hallway long before they come in. A chorus of bright and dark voices, they swirl together beneath the ceiling. The students grow quiet and shy as soon as they see me. A few of them come so close I can see their faces, corduroy moustaches, black capes lined with lambskin, their drilling eyes. They pinch my arm, poke at my eyes with their pens, as if they love me and they want to kill me. I long for the assistants' sugar cubes. The students glower at me, their staring faces squashed together in rows, all the way up to the railings under the ceiling, pinhead eyes. I boil in their magnetic gazes, suckle at their attention like a little child.

The professor asks: What is your name?
    I answer: Boy.
    Do you feel different from the other boys?
    I say: I draw on my moustache.
    The students laugh.
    They are a chorus.
    Different, different, they sing.
    I say: Then I look like the boys.
    The chorus cries: *Ha-ha-ha*.

The professor writes my initial: B. He writes Tara's last name on the blackboard. He writes a big X for my sex. I turn around in front of them. My shirt falls to the ground, I pull off my high leather boots and my pants, like I do before Tara's examinations. My little nipples, turned towards everyone's gaze, grow stiff. The professor, his fingers coloured with chalk and ink, runs his hand over the egg, and I shudder. The professor mumbles in confusion and quickly pulls his hand away, hurries to wash his fingers. His touch radiates through my skin, radiates far down my legs, makes me nauseous. I vomit little yellow pools across the floor, wipe my mouth with my hand. The assistants pat me on the back and tell me it's only nerves.

The faces turn to porridge, and all I see, far up in a distant row, is Tara's long coat and the frightful blood-red lining that billows around her. Tara's gaze shines through me. My body exudes its magic. My body spellbinds.

The assistants treat me kindly. Like an important person. They bring me more sugar cubes and tea on a tray. We take a break while I drink the dark, bitter tea. My knees are shaking. There is fire in my cheeks. Never before have I been so mighty. They turn their heads with my every movement. When I speak, they are silent. The delicate white cup in my hands. The gritty dregs of the tea. The big auditorium is cool and the students' voices are clear beneath the high ceiling: *Who are you?* they call to me curiously. *The unbaptized, the patient, the boygirl.* They draw caricatured sketches of me which they throw down to me by the lecture chair, and the crumpled papers land around me like sorrowful paper birds. Some of the boys have also drawn big, black ink hearts, which frame their taunting messages: *Let's meet outside at twelve o'clock. I'll buy you a dobos torte. Come on. We'll feed the pigeons. Don't tell anyone.*

Because I can't write, I whisper my replies as they pass, like the stupid little kid goat I am, and when they laugh at me, I know they never meant to take me away from here: *Help me. The truth is that I live with the boys. The truth is that I have an egg, but only the sisters have seen it. The truth is that I've kissed Beetle, but you must never tell Tara.*

One, two, three, and I'm closer to the darkness, which falls so quickly in February. The blizzard pulls at me. Over the forest the sky is watery and shining like a giant purple jellyfish. I am the chosen one. The one everyone wants to look at. The X-rays lift me up. The darkness inside the body has become visible. *Barium platinocyanide*. The magnetic field collapses. Lead and platinum are impenetrable for the rays. A bubbling euphoria. I am the centre of the auditorium. Of Dr Vajda's consultation room. Their eyes follow my every movement like fat flies. The men of science hunger. I beckon. All their eyes. I want to collect them and preserve them in Maria's jars.

In the house, where I am a little insect and a pale milk moustache and a coward because I no longer dare to kiss Beetle, the others still call me Boy. When I meet Beetle's mouth and feel his fingers crawl under my shirt, I'm afraid he will discover the wounds the rays have burned across my skin.

I boil sheets and pillowcases in the kitchen with Maria. She puts the great cast-iron pot on the stove, boils the fabric with blue soap and soda, and stirs. The water Maria dumps out on the front step dyes the snow a gleaming blue. I stumble on the threshold and scald one of my hands.

She pulls up my sleeve and sees my skin bubbling in great blisters where the rays hit. Red and yellow patterns, white splotches with pus, and in some places my skin is peeling off. Maria is shocked, she shuts me out in the snow and locks the front door behind me. I stay outside with my hand resting on the door handle.

Later Maria says: New York is in a fever over the rays. The great city. I see pictures of it in the newspaper, the towering buildings where people get sucked in and disappear. Steel and iron. People queue to be photographed, to get their own eternal portraits, to be illuminated by the rays: bones, head, hands, feet.

Dr Vajda from the X-ray clinic reaps praise from all over the world for his article about me. I imagine that the whole world is illuminated by the rays. That we can see wandering silhouettes with shining pink bones, nodding skulls, vague shadowy masses instead of flesh.

I tighten my shirt collar, put the black roses into a vase and prepare for dinner. Beetle carries the vinegar bowl around the table. He dips his big hands into it. He sways his hips slightly, sways a dance before me, pushes his hair away from his face. He whispers to me, he wants to know what I do with Tara. Where do you drive? What have you done? I can't tell him anything, but his questions drum on me like hail on a rooftop. Why can't I come too? I want to turn Beetle soft again, and I make the grimacing faces that usually get the boys to laugh. I steal boiled eggs from the kitchen and slip them into his lap during dinner. The soft, blue-white, peeled eggs are the finest gift I can think of, but he stares at me from across the table, his hands clutching silverware. He brings his fork to his mouth and twirls his knife in the air, twirls and twirls and twirls it inside my heart. Tells me: Nevermore.

I look down at my shiny tin plate, dizzy. A tear falls onto the plate and blends into the fat and the sauce. A tear calls for the highest punishment among the boys, but only Beetle sees it. He turns away. His face is stone. I have Dr Vajda's words in my head: *Don't be afraid. There are no secrets any more.* I have the professor's words in my head. The students' laughter. Beetle, I whisper, I want to tell you everything. But I can't. Tara would kill me. I am not like you. I will never be like you.

Who am I among the boys?

I am a night flyer.

The clock in the parlour strikes twelve.

Sleep is fitful in the purple room.

The pulsing of the moon.

The oily, oily skin.

The fever pounding in my blood keeps me awake.

A deep groan from within the house's stone walls. I steam in my own sweat, shaking. The boys lie in their beds in rows, faces turned down into their pillows. The geese are sleeping too, heads under wings. I rise from the bed, stand on my bare feet and feel the cold wash over my ankles. I'm watching you, Beetle. He lies on his side with his hands clasped, sleeping, his hair billowing across the sheet. The darkness is purple like the walls. He lies perfectly still, as if he were dead. His thin body curled in sleep. Soot on his eyelashes. There is a great yawn in time, and I want to reach down and touch him. I clutch the bars of his bed frame and lift my body, crawl onto the bed and over to Beetle. Don't worry about the boys. Don't worry about Tara and Maria. The moon is watching us. The starry sky's thousand pricks. The hoarse breathing of the others. Moonboy. Moongirl. I wake Beetle with a hand over his eyes, and, dazed, he welcomes me, moves over and makes room. We lie still beside each other. Not daring to move. Giggling, stiff as long wooden planks. What if the others hear us? The bed's frame parts the moonlight. There is a whirring in my ears. Listen here. Nothing will happen. We lie stretched in the darkness's singing. His breath, moving close to mine, the smell of cardamom and sweat, the blanket tickling my lip.

He brushes a hair from my cheek, and the warmth of his fingertip burns. We crash into each other with awkward elbows. We dig our way forward like moles, blind through layers of clothes. We unfasten the buttons of our shirts, push the hair out of each other's faces. Beetle fumbles above me, cautiously unties his pyjama bottoms, and they slide quickly over his thighs. And I pull mine down too, and now there is only our soft skin, whose light shines brighter than the moon.

I fill my lungs with air. Everything I have learned from Tara disappears. All of my upbringing: cold hands above the blanket, my bound chest. All that was held back opens. His face is soft, his eyelids half closed. You smell so good, he mumbles as he finds my nipples, which are stiff in the cold. His hand searches across my belly, which I tense.

Now he is lying on top of me, and breath flows fast through us, as if we were running.

We roll around and around, the sheet beneath us wet and hot, hair falling into our eyes. We see and hear only each other. We lie beside each other and atop each other like two stones. I over him, he over me. I am mighty, and I want more than him. We grope and lick each other like little kittens, I growl and purr. I pull teasingly at his hair, pull until he opens his mouth and his head arches back, pull until the lock of hair is mine. Ow, he says. Little devil. His cheek is so soft. I stroke his knees with my fingertips. I put my hand over his dangling flesh, and he puts his hand over my egg. We are the same movement, pressing back and forth.

The egg is hard and curved, it is turned towards him, but it doesn't open, though he rubs and presses with his fingertips to poke a hole in the flesh, as if searching for the seed inside a plum. He mashes his fingers into my skin, pokes and scrapes with his long nails so it hurts, and I feel his whole weight as he presses the breath out of me. I take hold of his narrow shoulders, dig my nails into his skin. And somewhere behind him floats the empty nightroom with the boys, somewhere behind him a key turns in the lock, and the door opens.

Then I look up. Tara in the night. A ghost. Our Red Mother reigns. I'm so scared I feel every single pore open to the night's icy air. My stomach muscles tense, prepared for a hit. There is Tara, transparent, and everything blows through her. But then she really is real, her flesh and her rage, her breath and her smell of alcohol and raw onions. Tall and straight in her dark-blue coat, the red silk lining billowing around her like a stream of blood. I see her so clearly, arms crossed, her gaze drilling through me, her disgust and disdain. Beetle and me in the bed send Tara into a rage. She has heard it, seen it. The red rage. I sing for her. I sing the name of her anger. Our Red Mother. It's no use. She clenches her hands into fists. Rapidly her chest rises and falls, her breath whistles. Her whole body is tense, her face blue with bulging blood vessels, her eyebrows thin, dark lines painted with a fine brush. She laughs. She turns away. Calls to the other boys. They sit up in their beds. They lick the purple light, which sits on their lips like glitter. They get up, they stand half naked in the room. They pick up the geese and hold them close. They crowd around us, they sing, and the one who sings the loudest is Sootmouth, who squints and spits a little gob from between his tightened lips. They see me as I am, naked, with Beetle. They see the egg. The boys draw closer as they clap and stomp. *Little moonboy came from heaven down to us, now we'll shake you until you're awake.* They take hold of the bed frame. Their eyes shine, there are purple rings around the irises.

Tara says I am unclean. She dunks my head into the water barrel, holds it down so long that I lose my breath. When I'm back on land, I gasp for air and stagger from side to side like a drunkard, and I know I can never again be like the light, white summer clouds or the bleached linen Maria hangs in the garden, if that's what Tara means by clean. Beetle gets away with it this time, for Beetle is not a night flyer, and the boys will forgive him, says Tara, but not me. But I am proud of myself. Though sobs sit in my throat and cold water runs from my hair down over my forehead, my eyes are dry as flour. No one will see me cry, even though it hurts somewhere between my ribs and a knife keeps on twirling and twirling in my heart. There are no secrets any more, my face is open and questioning in the reflection of the water barrel. My eyes are black pieces of coal. My eyes ask: Who am I?

BLEGDAM HOSPITAL
COPENHAGEN, 1952
(October)

Who am I? asked the biology teacher, and he pointed at the diagram. In the middle was a person drawn by Leonardo da Vinci. A study of proportions, he said, the harmonic forms of the Renaissance, the circle, the man inside, his navel at the centre, his arms stretched out from his body, his chest taut, the paper yellowed, and just below his navel, which is the centre of the circle, his genitalia: pubic hair, penis and testicles. The circle is the only thing that exists, the teacher says, and the empty circle is filled in with man, from which everything springs, and to which everything returns.

In class we dissected mice, pulled their long yellow and black entrails out of the opened bellies. One of the animals was pregnant. I cut open a female. The skinned creature lay in her red-lined coat with her mouth open, as if she were still calling for the little, living foetuses that fell from her belly and squeaked under the magnifying glass. I did not flinch as blood and slime covered the table. Only afterwards did I throw up.

I got my hands on an anatomy encyclopedia, I looked at the pictures of the man and the woman drawn beside each other: blood ears, blood faces and blood eyes, everything so clear and yet so strange that I grew dizzy. The woman slightly smaller than the man, tendons and muscles stretched to the limit, all skin scraped off. At first I was scared and I put the book away, but then I went back and picked it up, tore out the pages and hid them under my pillow until they seeped into the night and coloured my dreams red.

The television's great eye sparks, and we see Franz Ferdinand in his car: the camera zooms in on his chest, his face, the shadows under his eyes, his great, arched moustache. We see a vast plane of time, a woman shouting, the liberation, we see the Soviet Union's blockade of Berlin, 1948–49, the Zschornewitz power plant shut down on Soviet orders, we see milk loaded onto a plane bound for West Berlin, the airlift, planes in rows at Tempelhof, great dark birds, we hear the clinking of the milk bottles. We see a ballet, we see the dancer Vaslav Nijinsky dressed as the puppet Petrushka, we see him dancing in Berlin, in Budapest, in Paris, in Rio, in New York long before the borders were closed, we watch him dancing as a woman, dancing as a man, skin stiff with make-up and enormous eyelashes. The announcer lady says he was the most famous dancer, that his leap was a leap into freedom. We see Red Rosa, Rosa Luxemburg, shot and thrown into the waters of the Landwehrkanal, we see Rosa in the steel-grey water, eyes open, and the gleam of the test pattern, we see the Danube, shining and blue, we who disappear ourselves, we see the river.

Ella shows me photographs of herself and the man. They're standing in Mother's garden, in the shadow of the oak tree. Mother was the one who took the picture. Ella smiles when she tells me about the deception. No one in the photograph is smiling, they stare stubbornly into the camera, holding out their glasses of dark whisky and ice cubes towards the photographer. Ella told Mother that the man was a student training to be a woodworker, that all they do together is study maths. Nothing more. Ella had a birthday party and Mother let her use the house, said she could have a few girlfriends over, not her new friend. She shows me another picture, one she took: a table of empty bottles, full ashtrays, half-eaten plates of food, a bowl of raisins, beer bottles, crumpled wrapping paper. The man sits bent over on our sofa, completely closed off, not looking at the camera. The angle is a little crooked. We were drunk, Ella says, giggling. We lay down in Mother's bedroom, took off our clothes. He's my little secret.

We held hands on the way to the cinema, and in the darkness, in the soft polyester seats, I watched his face, which pictures flickered across and made so strange and beautiful. I had to look away, gasping for air. When I looked up at the screen again the reel was whirring, the beams of light flickering. I felt so dizzy. He gave me a present as the credits rolled: a watch. It's so pretty, with a light-blue band, and I put it on right away, look.

Ella says: Agnes.
　　Yes?
　　It's the right thing. I know it.
　　What is?
　　To be with him.
　　Only with him.
　　Now I understand, says Ella.
　　Sitting so close to him in the darkness, so close we breathe in time with each other.
　　Do you understand?
　　The smell of his cologne, sweat.
　　Holding his hand.
　　It's hard to be here, Agnes.
　　It smells so strange here.
　　It's so quiet here.
　　It's hard, when someone is calling to me. Tugging at me with his whole body. Tugging at me like a melody that plays again and again, that I've just got to hear.
　　And you. You know nothing. Really nothing.

Ella lifts the pencil from the paper. She says she can't go on this way. I don't believe in it, I don't believe you, she says. Defiant. Furrowed brow. Ella says that the man says it's all made up. Lies. Ella raises her voice, even though I say ssh, shush her, say: No, no, you mustn't leave. Ella says: I'm tired of it all, of you, of your story, of coming here, breathing the smell of bleach and piss, of illness when I myself am healthy. I'm tired of sitting here day after day. Then go, I say, and Ella stands from her chair so fast it falls over, and the nurses come running into the room to see what's happened. Ella runs out of the room, disappearing down the corridor.

Last night I saw my lungs floating outside myself. They hung over me in the hospital room like two smoke-filled balloons. They were beautiful, draping the empty air. In fact, they were one of the most beautiful things I've seen. The blood vessels were illuminated, purple and blue, splintering through the thin membrane. The lungs gave off a grumbling, buzzing sound. They smelled like camphor. Suddenly I could move freely, and I stretched my arms towards the ceiling as far as I could. I tried to reach out for the lungs, but a strange mechanism, thin as a knitting needle, raised them higher every time I reached out my arms. I tried to suck in air but I couldn't, there was only the sound of the leather membrane, which slammed shut in the iron lung like a set of false teeth.

Dreams converge: the iron lung is my armour, my hair is aflame. I can stand up and move inside my green metal sheath. I move through landscapes of iron-green moss. I battle time with my sword, cast my gaze into the future like a ray.

When the pain gets bad, they sedate me with ether. They say it's good for me. I see strips of coloured paper flapping before my face. A great, shining lake. Ether, the heavenly substance, son of night and darkness.

Today the nurses rolled me outside. They pushed me carefully out of the iron lung, pulled me out on the metal stretcher, and for a second I thought they were going to let me go. It's October, but it's still warm. The air was so soft against my skin. The leaves, which are now yellow, drifted down onto my white sheet. The sun was sharp, it spotted my pupils. I lay under the open sky and birds circled above my head. Exhaust from the road seeped into my lungs. I thought of Ella, how she was walking around somewhere out in the city, in the bright squares, under the heavy, orange rays of the autumn sun, skipping so gracefully over the storm drains that everyone turns their heads. Who was that? A girl, a young woman, on the way to her lover. I thought of how she was walking without me. On the way to the man. Away from me. Then I heard a scream. I grew frightened. The scream sliced the air, cut through my bones. And I realized the scream was coming from me. I told the nurses to roll me inside again, I told them I never wanted to see the world outside the hospital again. Here in the sickroom everything is clear. Now it is here, and nowhere else, I want to be. I turn myself towards myself, and I watch.

TARA'S HOUSE, 1913

(carnival)

A scream flays the air. It is carnival. We sing. Tomorrow is Ash Wednesday, and we've been waiting for it. Today Maria does the butcher's work. She gets one of the sheep from the red stable, ties it to a wooden post in the garden, and we receive no warning before she walks out of the kitchen with a knife, before the knife is lodged into its throat. We have no time to duck before we hear the sheep's scream, and the blood streams, drenching its fleece. The scream sits in the walls, in our ear canals, in our bones.

Carefully, carefully she cuts away the skin, a tight grip around the knife. The entrails spill out, the burst blue membranes, the pulsating black and yellow strands. The blood melts into the snow.

The smell of the blood is so strong it flows through the windows, presses through the house's walls and sits in our clothes.

Tara rinses the skin in the water barrel and leaves it to cure in a tub of the sisters' urine. The fat floats to the surface, green. The sisters go out every other hour and spread their legs above the tub, lift their skirts, crouch down and pee, water the skin to make it soft, to make it strong. The fat from the fur floats to the surface, green.

The sheep head is dangling from a hook below the stable's roof, the teeth grinning yellow. Fog from the forest enfolds it. It is carnival, and the winter's demons must be driven out.

The boy's eyes are hard, round balls, they hang greedily on Maria and Tara as they boil the sheep's bones. We sit around the table, all of us, the boys from the purple room and the yellow room, and I sit there with them too. Little insect. All the things they call me. Whore. Pigboy. Tin canboy. Nevermore-boy. The words they sneer through their teeth. They know what happened between Beetle and me. Tara knows it. The house knows it, and the walls know it, and they close around us, muttering.

Tara turns and places her hand on Beetle's neck, pulls him close. I stare at Beetle, make faces and bat my eyelashes, and I want to say: Look at me. Hold me. But his eyes are glazed, he casts them down. I know he is afraid of Tara, afraid of the boys. He sits beside Sootmouth, skinny Sootmouth with the cold eyes. Sootmouth who I kissed in the forest, vile kisses. The two of them jab each other with their elbows, laugh. Long, cold fingers creep up my throat. I want to let the hounds loose and run into the forest. I want to empty all of Tara's schnapps bottles and Maria's pillboxes. Spin around, whirl like the curtains in the breeze, stretch every muscle until I get dizzy and forget. The house. Tara. The boys. And yet I keep on staring, I want to cut out his tongue and lick the salt from his fingertips. Beetle sits down between the other boys, who make room for him. He smiles to them, his hair shining brilliantly on his head.

It is carnival. We sing. The boys' faces beam. For today I am a part of their circle again. Today, and only today, because of the celebration. The boys cut the teeth out of the sheep head, drill holes in them, string them onto a thread. It is carnival, and for today I am one of them.

Maria makes glue, crushes and grinds the bones to a soft, white powder in the mortar, mixes it with water in a pot. The water boils all day, steam billowing around her. We lift the lid, and when most of the water has evaporated, she forms it into little glowing clumps of amber, beads of bone between her hands.

Tara boils oil in little pans, rolls sweet dough into long rolls, cuts it up with scissors, joins the ends to make rings, and lets the dough simmer in the fatty oil. She fishes out the rings, fills them with apricot marmalade and sprinkles them with sugar. Tara fills her glass with cherry schnapps and empties it again. She pours glasses for us, too, the older boys. We raise our glasses high up to the ceiling and swallow the sweet, yeasty drink.

Maria dissolves the little amber beads from the bones in water and they turn to sticky glue. We cut masks out of wood, cut breathing holes for our mouths and noses and little holes for our eyes, paint big, grinning mouths, red lips, red cheeks. We glue on strips of lambswool for hair, long, soft wigs. We sit around the table with our masks on. We are all giddy from the scent of the glue in the pot, from the sugar and the sweet apricots, which glitter in droplets at the corners of our mouths.

Then the other boys yell: Fire! Sootmouth points at me and says: Not you. They storm down the hall with the younger boys, they tie their boots.

I stand in the parlour by the window and watch the boys in the forest. They have their masks on. They form a circle, tall columns in their woollen coats, clouds of breath. They've borrowed the big saw from Tara, and there are two on each side of it: they use all their weight, moving it rhythmically back and forth. They sing: *Now the tree shall fall, now the tree shall fall with a bang*, until the trunk begins to tilt. A screeching hiss as the tree hits the ground. The littlest boys walk along the forest edge, bent over, gathering branches and twigs, gathering birch switches, wobbling back with their heavy loads to stack them up alongside the house. They tie the switches into bundles, singing all the while.

> *O little frog, I'm taking you,*
> *quack-quack, quack-quack, quack-quack.*
> *My three hungry children are waiting for you,*
> *quack-quack, quack-quack, quack-quack.*

I wait for the boys for the rest of the day. They rustle at the edge of the forest. The house's shutters bang in the cold wind. They come back from the forest late in the evening. Beetle is with them. I take off my clothes in the too-small wardrobe, pull my nightshirt over my head, fold my clothes and place them under my bed. I hear the boys giggle out in the darkness, pull off their boots, pet the geese. Sweat and the sharp smell of oily skin fills the air.

The sound of a bell in the middle of the night. It rings so clear and glassily in the darkness. A narrow yellow crack opens, like an eye. Tara's bell. The white geese are restless. The bell rings the house awake. A magnetic whirring in the walls. I open my eyes, but I can't see Tara. I can only see the boys, who are standing around me in a circle. I've been expecting them. Now they're here. They've stolen Tara's bell. They hold it up. The purple walls shine. My skin shines. The boys' heads come closer. They've put on their woollen coats and masks. Beetle stands among them, I recognize his slender form. I know who you are behind the mask.

The boys are in a silent fervour. Little sparks fly off them, a quiet buzzing. They bring me a certainty: I can no longer remain in the house. They have the birch switches in their hands, and they start to hit me, spitting. The switches break my skin. The boys open their clenched fists and cast ashes onto me. They rub the ashes into the cuts.

Beetle is among them. It really is him. He is the one who hits the hardest, who kicks me, who drags me out of my bed. The boys pull the sheet off me. It is stained with my blood. They herd me down the hall, quiet so as not to wake Maria, not to wake Tara. I want to call out to Tara, but I've lost my voice. I squeak like a little mouse and no one hears me, no one comes to see. The boys already know what's about to happen, the whole house knows it, the house breathes anxiously through its silent walls, and no one can stop it.

We are in the garden. The night clings like oil to my skin. I tremble. The boys stand in a circle around me, they mutter and hum. They plunge my head into the water barrel, pull me up again, and I gasp for air. They drag me onward, laughing, to the tub of urine where the sheepskin is soaking. They press my head down into the awful fluid until the urine drains the oxygen from my lungs.

When I come to again the boys have undressed me, they've pulled me out of my shirt, they've gathered the birch switches into a pile in the garden. They stack the firewood from the day's work on top. They hold me tight and take turns sitting beside me, they lick my face like the hounds. They cut off my hair, grab it by the roots and pull. Clumps fall to the ground one after another, and the boys rub their hands over my stubbly scalp. Sootmouth goes into the red stable and comes back out with a pair of tongs. He bashes them against the windowpanes of the stable and the hounds start barking. Another boy comes out of the house with a piece of glowing firewood. The boys tie up the hounds, muzzle their jaws with the rope. The hounds hang silently on their leashes, lunging with quick jolts, pulling their throats long and blue.

The boys light a fire. The red tongues dance. The boys take turns feeding the flames. They throw great, heavy logs through the air. The embers blaze. With every breath I taste the blue smoke, something sweet, terrible. The snow melts in a ring around the flames, and the fire singes the grass. They heat the tongs in the fire. The flames advance, the heat beats out and burns blisters on our faces. I close my eyes. The boys laugh at me, take turns coming up to pinch my arms, between my legs. They give Beetle the tongs, he holds them close to the coals, steps forward. Two of the other boys hold me down. I writhe. Beetle takes hold of one of my swells, grips it with the tong, and with his face turned away, as I spit and call for the hounds and call for Tara, he tears off one nipple and then the other. The pain is a long thread going up my spine, arresting all senses. I go into a ring of fire.

I wake up beside the water barrel. It is still dark, ruffled moonlight, little veined eggs of light on the grass. I look across the hoed potato patch, look to the house, where the lights are burning, but the boys have disappeared. No one is awake in the house. I slide in and out of consciousness, dormant. I can no longer feel any pain, my skin is like a thick cape, senseless, swaddling my skeleton and my organs. The boys have untied the hounds. They run restlessly around me, lick my face.

I lift the sheep head from the hook on the stable roof and pull its skin out of the tub of urine. I hollow out the head with the tongs, dig out the eyes so there are holes for my own eyes, pull the head over my own head and drape the skin around me. Urine runs from the fleece onto my skin and dries into a sticky membrane. I throw my old clothes on the embers, awakening the flames, which dance across the fabric and swallow it at once. Only my tall brown leather boots remain, and I pull them onto my feet. I turn my back on the house. Vanish from the garden and the house's circle of light. I pick up a glowing branch from the fire and call to the hounds. As soon as they hear my voice, they creep across the grass, they follow me. I walk with them along the river, into the forest.

THE PASSAGE

I am in the forest. Someone is calling me from deep within, waiting for me, yet the forest is completely silent. Maybe it is the forest itself which takes me in, comforts me, swaddles me in its damp air. The sheepskin clings tightly to my skin, and even though the fleece is wet, it is light to carry. At first there is a cool, earthy smell, an embrace. Soft, rotting leaves, thickets and spiderwebs. The trunks of the trees are illuminated by a thin, red light that comes from the earth, not from the sky. I follow the river a while, further into the forest. I make a hole in the ice with a stone and drink the freezing water.

It is bleeding where my nipples were torn, the blood drips into the snow. I am dizzy. When I lie down on the cold, white floor, I look up between the trunks. The needles of the fir trees sprinkle down on me, snow and earth soak up my blood. Shadows wrap themselves around me like a tent, dew beads on my bones. Skin can be torn off, peeled off slowly, one nail after another, dwindling to nothing, to a purity like a polished, chalk-white skull. I stand up and walk.

The hounds follow me, they lie down a few metres from me, they are always watchful, and they follow me with their eyes, lick my face when I finally fall asleep. The rest of the night passes quickly, a breath of cold soil, stars and darkness.

When the morning comes, I hear the sisters calling for the hounds, calling: Boy. Boy, where are you? Come back to us. I can feel the hounds' fear. The sisters' cries reach me deep in the forest. The hounds prick their ears, they sniff. Some part of them wants to obey, to bound off towards the sisters' voices. The hounds stand up. I hear them bark, sniff around between the tree trunks, I see their eyes shine. But they turn around, they come back to me.

I walk for days. Through the forest, towards the city. The dark of night disquiets me. Sometimes I get so scared that I disappear into myself, under the skin, aware of nothing but my own blood, which crashes through my veins. Other times I cocoon myself in fear, sounds are amplified, branches creak drily, leaves rustle, surround me with a thousand whispering voices. I quake.

The forest closes itself around me. The long shadows crown me, branches whip the sheepskin. The pains come slowly back, jabbing me, buzzing under my skin, leading me over the ground. My sores stiffen as the days go by. The hollows where my nipples were grow knotty and black. My skin sucks the blood and the wound back into itself. My skin grows slowly, grafts onto the sheepskin in a stiff, brittle layer, like resin. The final days of February, the first days of March, when light thunders through the branches. New little shoots of screaming green. The scabs fall off, and the strangest mounds of flesh swell from my chest. My bare skin under the sheepskin hardens, and my hands and ankles are covered in cuts, scratches and mosquito bites. The sheepskin clings to my flesh, crawls and stretches like long, tickling fingers, caresses my flesh, caresses the purple, blue, red. Layers of fat grow and grow, dissolve and meld, until it is almost impossible to see where the rough, woolly skin meets the tissues of my body, just a knobbly yellow band.

I lick bark to collect the dew, turn pine cones around in search of fat seeds, knock white larvae from the bark with a big rock, and they answer me, throng out to meet me.

Hunger drills into me, makes me feeble and heedless of dangers. I suckle from a goat tied up in front of a forest cabin built of wide, newly tarred beams. The yard is empty. The tar fumes in the sun. The goat is skinny, there are open sores on its neck. The door is ajar. I see a shadow move inside the house, a man yells loudly, and I run. I run, run, until I fall to the forest floor. My pulse is heavy throughout my body.

I eat the berries frozen to the branches of ash trees and dig up squirrels' hoards. I gather pine cones and stand with them in my hand. They look like little hibernating animals, curled up silently in my palm.

I sleep in the treetops, crawl up and hold on tight. I gnaw at the bitter bark, my stomach turns, and I vomit yellow pools. The hounds lie waiting by the tree's roots. I am soft. I expose my organs under glittering stars.

By early spring I've come so far that I can see the lights of the city, a membrane of dust and noise, of flickering sulphur lights. I crawl down from the trees, moving through a silent, irradiated zone, a place for neither people nor animals. The withered foliage parts and a blue light flutters over the fields. I take short, cautious steps, as if seeing the world for the first time, as if I am only now mature enough to see and know. I tramp and stagger through the boggy ground as if my feet were hooves, walk the last stretch through the forest, through the thinning thicket. I can see the river again, it grows wider as the forest ends, fills with blue water, forms itself to its stony quay, a metallic, glittering mirror. The river flows, full of the city's rubbish: crumpled newspapers, potato peelings, ashes. Bones and entrails thrown into the water by the butchers. It whirs through my body. I feel the river's magnetic pull. I walk towards the city.

BUDAPEST, 1913

(DICTIONARY)

Pearl of the Danube. The Danube: the blue river. The river is called Donau in German, it is called Dunaj in Slovakian, Donava in Slovenian, Dunărea in Romanian and in Hungarian Duna. The city is known for its mills and factories, for its nightlife and its brothels, its taverns and clubs. It is the beginning of the twentieth century, war is on the horizon, yet people plaster up their facades and build new buildings, full of hope, cut up their dresses and sew new ones from the same fabric.

They're performing Strauss's *Elektra* at the Vienna Court Opera when the shots are fired in Sarajevo. Gavrilo Princip points the pistol (a Browning FN model 1910) at the carriage where Franz Ferdinand sits, he shoots twice, and the war to end all wars begins. Budapest is the easternmost capital of the great Austro-Hungarian Empire, which will be split in two, though no one knows it yet. In Budapest there is still peace. The city lies in a pink fog. The river sparkles: on the Buda side is Gellért Hill with the citadel, on the flat Pest side are the parliament, businesses and the grey administrative buildings, the boulevards and vast residential areas. You can get lost in its streets. The city has 880,000 inhabitants. It is spring in Budapest and the wind tugs kerchiefs from the pedestrians. The city lies open. It is waiting.

THE DARKNESS AND
THE LIGHT
BUDAPEST, 1913

(newborn)

The lamplighters walk around and open the darkness under the yellow, rose and purple sky, they wander with their long poles in the centre of the city. The hounds are my tail of shadows.

The city sucks me in. I disappear down narrow streets.

When I reach the river, the city unfolds. A low rushing of water. Soft, purple mountains rising. The houses that climb the mountain's spine cast green shadows. I stand beneath an acacia tree, blue and dripping with condensation, and I want to touch everything with my eyes, touch the people who live here. I climb down to the quay, under a bridge that crosses the river, and I wrap my arms around the great piles, lean my body against them as if they were other enormous bodies. Mist rises from the water. Through the mist the water is yellow and blue like a gas flame. I lick up the water with my eyes, let the river run through me and fill me up.

I see a girl walking along the quay and follow her for a while. She has a long coat on and braided hair, a big felt bag she drags over the ground, so big, as if there were a person inside. Before the light returns, she slides into the blueblack membrane of the night.

The bar is further down the river. The hounds lead the way there. At first they dart about, sniff at the gutters, sense with their tails, then they pick up the scent of a back courtyard. They dig through stinking rubbish bins. A waft of rat-tails disappears under the bins. Low barracks. A great building of shiny, soft, rounded bricks. A red neon sign over a narrow black doorway in the building: THE ELECTRIC PALACE. It is almost morning, but the bar is still open. I hear laughter. The first light glitters on the river. The red neon sign pulsates. THE ELECTRIC PALACE. The name is so full of hope, of something new. I don't know what awaits me. Whether the place is dangerous for me. But my hunger pushes me onwards. Hunger for people, hunger for food. I open the door.

A reddish fog of smoke and alcohol. Figures deep in the fog move back and forth, dance rhythmically, appear and vanish again. Soft, elastic laughter. Spots of light on faces. Hands folded around each other. It is so warm here, so full of people, that condensation gathers in big drops on the walls. The drops cling to the sheepskin. Smells of rose water, of sweat, of the dark waters of the river.

The bar is decorated with red and purple fabric, the bar and the walls, red and purple everywhere: the curtains, the cushions, the tablecloths, the wrappers of the sweets sitting in a great glass vase on the bar. Velour and tulle, thinly woven cotton and smooth silk, shining leather stretched across the seats. Everything is woven together in shades of red, and only the bouquet of paper lilies by the entrance is white.

Faces appear and vanish again in the smoky fog, the faces wear make-up, the eyes are searching, coal eyes, red lips. Scattered phrases. *Hey, do you have a cigarette? Little darling. Come on. I'm doing much better. I'm getting out and about.* My body sloshes in turmoil. The big, swaying sheep head has grown heavy. The fur curls over my belly, over my shoulders, bluish with mould. The wool is falling out in clumps, and the skin smells so strong that I'm worried they'll throw me out. But I want to answer them, touch their faces, their soft skin and hair, their painted lips, and through the fog that fills the room, so thick that it seems to have risen from the river, I want to shout: Here I am.

May I have a glass of milk? I ask at the bar, mustering all my courage: Nothing more, just a big glass of warm milk. I bow my head. Fear rushes through me, yellow and clear, like urine. I don't know anyone here. What if they don't like me? Maybe they'll throw me out, rip off my nails, cut off my arms and legs, throw me in the river like rubbish. Be kind. Give me warmth. Take me as I am. The bartender is tall and lanky, his head hanging low between his shoulders, high cheekbones, dark curly hair. He glances over at me. He has big hands with pretty rings on them. The stones are different colours, violet, dark green, blue. At first he refuses to serve me. It seems like he wants to push me out of the door. He turns towards another customer. I want to turn around and leave too. My legs grow soft, I tremble, cry big, shiny, eternal tears through the eyeholes in the sheep head. I am alone. All alone in the big, unknown city. I duck down until my tears have run dry, wipe the eyeholes with the back of my hand and listen to the calming buzz of the voices. Ask again: Warm milk. The bartender raises his eyebrows, looks me up and down, flicks a cigarette butt off the bar. You can sit here, but only while you drink your glass of milk, he says, disappearing behind the bar.

I hold the cup with both hands for warmth, drink the milk in great, greedy gulps. When I hold my hands in front of my face, they are shaking. For a moment I think I hear the hounds barking outside.

Thank you, I say. I summon my courage and ask: What's your name?

He smiles, finally he smiles, and his smile licks up my cheek like a warm flame. Aliz, he says. I look at him, whisper the name to myself so I won't forget it. A real name. A name from Budapest. Aliz. Aliz. Aliz.

Someone holds out a cigarette case and I pull out a cigarette, timid. Someone offers me a glass of beer, comes closer, holds out their hands. Rough tongues. Nails yellowed from tar and tobacco. Fingers wreathed in big rings, like Aliz's. They touch the sheepskin, look at me inquisitively, tug mouldy tufts from the skin, wrinkle their noses at the smell. I curl up on the chair, afraid of what they might do to me.

Let's talk a little while.

Do you want a beer?

Do you smoke?

Aliz drums his fingers on the bar, hums a song. I look down into my cup. Suddenly I feel so soft. All my nerves have drained away. Aliz taps a fresh keg, pours a big mug and pushes it over to me. I take a sip. It is yellow as grain, it tastes bitter. The other guests leave me be. I mimic their careless, elegant movements, wave my cigarette, emit a few soft sounds, cough, inhale again, pull the dry smoke down into my lungs. I take a great gulp of beer, which foams in my mouth. I lean my head back and laugh, the way the others do, but inside the sheep head it sounds like a strange sob.

Then the lights come on above the stage. A group of dancers. They stand in a ring. Long eyelashes like little paintbrushes. Tight corsets and short skirts, smooth suits that stick to their bodies like fish skin. Ribs and hip bones. Shining pageboy haircuts, sharp kohl eyes, their faces held high up over their shoulders, tilted up at the ceiling. The dancers' ring opens. In the middle is a woman in a long, white jacket and white trousers. She steps into the sharp spotlight. Her hair is pulled back tightly and gathered into a ponytail. She has a serious face, which glistens with oil. Her eyebrows two great arches, like a melancholy Pierrot: a big, beautiful, white clown. A great moustache painted above her lips. The woman starts to sing as she moves across the stage, and the dancers spread out around her like a fan. A deep voice from far inside the bar's darkness flows high up in the air, up where the electric wires are strung.

I feel my body grow warm, loosen, and I want to laugh. I can be here. Here in this room. Borne by the dancers' movements. Arms, braided into one another, meander, as light and pliant as snakes, and grab out for me. Sticky smells of perfume, of chemical powders and leather. The dancers bow before the singer. Her mouth is round and soft. Her face smooth and magnetic.

I become light as a crisp autumn leaf as I watch her inky upper lip, and I really think the singer is smiling at me under that thin, winding line.

I forget the hounds waiting for me outside. I forget where I've come from, the house in the forest, Tara, Maria and the boys. The cold walls. The thoughtless hands, red slaps. The stiff, white shirts that sucked the air from my lungs, tied up my breath. The boys. Stiff at night with their arms over the blanket. Their hands clapping now-you-will-die. The heat of the fire, which melts the skin. Everything covered in a wet sheet, a white vinegar veil. Mummies. And now: a whirring deep inside my body. A swarm of flies batting about under my skin. The laughter of the guests, the colours, all the glowing shades of red. The singer's soft, deep tones lure her audience in.

> *Like a dog at the tidewaters,*
> *like a ghost fluttering through a thousand years.*
> *I am on the hunt, I shoot doves from the rooftops.*
> *Cars slice up the sky,*
> *Build a gambling hall, a casino in my head,*
> *of glistening purple and red.*
> *Do you know where we are now?*
> *In Budapest.*

A little group comes in, sparkling billows of frosty blue air around them. They stand at the bar, greet each other, kiss cheeks, kiss hands. They are different from the other guests, who have come in their work clothes: jackets and uniforms, flat shoes with laces, long woollen skirts. They lean across the bar, indifferent to who might be watching them. Some wear long black jackets with tails reaching all the way to their ankles, like in a funeral procession. Carnations in their buttonholes. Cigars. Monocles. Heavy make-up, wide eyes. As if they were performing in a circus.

One of the young women from the group makes her way towards me. In high-heeled shoes, a brown woollen coat, a corduroy cap. A yellow aster tickles her chin. Her skin shines like zinc, her eyes are marked with knife-thin stripes of kohl. She leans over the bar, bobs her head so her hair falls like a dark ray. The bar's red light clings to her face, makes it look pretty and smooth and mask-like. Absinthe-green eyes. She wears a buttoned-up shirt under her coat. A warmth hits me. Is she looking at me? She doesn't move.

The woman wrinkles her nose like the others. She leans towards me, runs her fingertips over the sheepskin inquisitively. I jolt, and she takes a step back. Why do you look like that? Is it a costume? she asks. She cocks her head again and stares at me: It's original, in any case. I bow my head, shy. She says that she's a dancer. That she knows the singer, Irma. That she has danced for Irma. That she lives here, above the Electric Palace. She says that she doesn't dance any more. That there are more important things now. She has a leather bracelet of enamel beads around her wrist. The beads clink when she moves. The soot from her eyes is smudged down her cheeks. A smell of smoke, of hunger and sleeplessness.

She lights a cigarette, smiles yellowly. Her thin wrists and her cigarette circling. The song of her bracelet. What's your name?

Boy.

Boy, she repeats. That's not a name.

She raises her eyebrows.

Lulu, she says. My name's Lulu.

What are you doing here in the city? she asks.

I'm looking for a place to sleep.

Lulu laughs.

Every bed is a home for a night.

Lulu looks around the room. I haven't slept in a day. Been travelling, she says. Just got home. Vilnius, Berlin, Prague. But now the day is dawning. The day can last forever. You look tired. You look like you've never been in a bar before. We need a beer.

Yes, I say.

There was snow everywhere I travelled, real snow. Lulu bends towards me, opens her eyes wide. The fields were white. But it wasn't really real. Just dust, sun, ash, burning fields. The trains stopped, carriages burned, boiled like pots in the heat of the fires. The cars were full of soldiers coming from training. They were packed in like herrings. They stared. They looked right through me. Caked with mud. They stank in their woollen uniforms. I opened my bag and gave them bread. I gave them milk.

I say: Vilnius, Berlin, Prague. I taste the words.

I think of Lulu on the train and Lulu in the cities. She glows from within, all illuminated, whiteyellow.

Lulu says: In every city I found a bed for a night.

The beer foams gently in my mouth, I pull the carbon dioxide in through my nose. A soft pounding in my cheeks. I look over at Aliz, who is hanging over the bar, waving his rings. I lower my head. I'm on guard, I can hear every voice in the room. I'm afraid that Aliz will finally find me out. An intruder. Carrion. But he looks the other way, kisses a customer, a man in a light cotton suit and a dark hat. He also has a little carnation in his buttonhole. They stand on their toes to reach one another, hands on each other's necks, circling tongues, spit. They are indifferent to the rest of us. I feel lucky. I inhale Lulu's scent, her sour breath, the tar from the cigarette she's smoking, the sweat that soaks her shirt in great, dark rings. Her perfume, a faint whiff of incense, vanilla, cinnamon.

And then Prague, says Lulu. After Vilnius, after Berlin, Prague. The bridges and the river in Prague. The river was a blood vessel running through the city, a quiet, bubbling pulse. In Prague she changed clothes, brushed her teeth for the first time in months. A secret meeting. There were five of us in all, Lulu says. Including a man called Leo, who climbed up onto a beer keg, stood there waving his arms, and though there were only a handful of them there, he was so passionate, and it was night-time and everyone else was sleeping, but they were awake, and it felt like everyone ought to be awake that night. I'm talking about the society, says Lulu, the society we can shape like a clump of clay, form, glaze and fire.

Lulu sighs.

I ask: What is a society?

Lulu licks her fingers. Laughs at me.

Lulu says: You've got a lot to learn.

Lulu says: A revolution is like a child. The child must live, yet you fear it will die.

I say: What if I'm already dead?

Lulu pinches my arm, and I flail in the chair. You see. Alive. But what's the matter? Are you crying? Your eyes are so red. She caresses my hand. Lulu is warm. Full of something hopeful and porous. She isn't like the sisters in the house. Not like Tara, serious and tall. Not like Maria, soft as dough, meek in her bed, coughing up tar from her mouth. Not at all like Beetle, shy, timid, cold and pale. She is not afraid of anything. Lulu is overflowing, she clicks her tongue, flicks her cigarette butt, her teeth strong and yellow, grinning. I touch her hand cautiously. Her skin is soft butter that my fingertips sink into. She orders me warm milk with rum, orders me several glasses. You seem so young. One day you'll grow to be something bigger than yourself. Society. Community, says Lulu. The milk streams through me. Lulu's words. Big and jagged and wild. I feel warmth move through my body for the first time since I left the house, slowly spreading inside my bones, the blood flowing up in my cheeks, under the sheepskin. I slip down from the chair, step into the red light that hangs over the floor like a great, soft flag, and walk lightly, as if I weren't wearing boots, between the people dancing.

A woman is sitting beside me on the floor, holding my hand. I've been sleeping. It must be morning. Thin threads of light. I lie on a mattress in a little attic room with worn floorboards. It's practically empty. There is only one window up by the rafters. It stands ajar. A shabby, green sofa covered with a yellow sheet. In the corner there is a little coal stove, a sack of coal and a box of matches. The woman gets up and shovels coal into the oven. She opens the vent, strikes a match. The noxious smell of sulphur fills the air. The flames eat their way across the coals.

I listen for the hounds, but the courtyard is quiet. The cold night air blows in. It smells of melted snow and soil, sharp and fresh. I pull away from the woman, crawl across the floor and curl up in the ashes by the stove, afraid of what the woman might do. Beat me, throw me out.

She is skinny. Her hair is braided down her back. Her deep voice blows away the membranes of sleep and dreams. A voice that pulls at me, sucks me in. I saw you down in the crowd. Lulu poured rum into you, didn't she? You passed out. We carried you up here.

When she bends down over me, I recognize her as the singer from the stage, the great white clown, but her face is washed clean. Little spots of make-up and oil still sit along her hairline. Her hands lie warm on my chest. It's as if her voice is also touching me, in the same way her hands do. The woman has on a pair of rough linen trousers and a checked shirt. She says that her name is Irma, that she is from the other side of the Atlantic Ocean, from the city of San Francisco, that she owns this place.

What's your name?
    I'm just a little insect, a kid goat.
    It sounds like a promise.
    Where are you from?
    I come from the forest.
    Are the dogs yours?
    No.
    Irma says: They made so much noise. I let them out.
    I say: May I stay here a while?

Irma strokes my head with her hand, strokes the big sheep head, and I think to myself that she probably has no idea who she has let in, a boy who washes rage into the cheeks of one and all, because she moves her hand in rhythmic movements, touching me through the thick layer of skin and fat and hair without being shy or afraid.

Irma returns at dusk with Lulu and Aliz. Aliz has a penknife and a little lantern, and they start cutting the fleece. They work together, sitting on their knees. Irma cuts, and Aliz and Lulu bite and tug at the skin. The smell of mouldy sheepskin poisons the room. I jolt whenever I feel the tip of the knife against my skin, until finally it releases me with a sucking sound, without blood, without pain. The skin takes all my body hair with it. I am covered in a yellow, scaly layer, which smells bitter, like glue. Lulu drags a big tub into the room and Irma fills it with warm water and a dark-yellow oil that pearls on the surface. Steam rises, white in the cold air. The three of them gather around me, expectant, silent, solemn. I surrender myself to their hands, step into the water. Irma soaps me, the oily soap foams, she holds my head between her hands with a firm grip and dunks it under. Water closes over my head. Irma pulls me up again, right before I run out of air, and uses a ladle to rinse away the soap before they take me out of the water, rub me dry and swaddle me. A shiver runs through my body. I look down at myself. My skin is completely new: smooth, blue-specked and hairless like a newborn.

I open myself to my new name, which Irma gives me: from the girls' name Ignatia and the boys' name Ignatius. Iggy.

TIME

(DICTIONARY)

Chronology (from the Greek χρόνος, chronos, meaning 'time', and λόγος, logos, meaning 'word, reason') is the reason for the divisions of time. The god of time, Chronos (χρόνος), is the origin of Chaos.

Time is the water that streams. Time is the river. The water that whirls and circles and parts into smaller streams and riverbeds. The river that streams or dries out, that changes shape along the quays and the muddy banks. The soft, sludgy river bottom. Time sucks everything in and lets it go again, faces and bodies, hands and feet, organs, it washes the bodies clean.

Time is also the dark-blue linen threads of Franz Ferdinand's uniform at the Museum of Military History in Vienna, wrinkled in the dry breeze of the ventilator. The body falls through the uniform and dissolves. The blood keeps running from the crown prince's mouth. His eyelids quiver. Very little of the body remains smeared on the stiff fibres, only the dry blood, a splash of brown and red sucked into the weave. Time is the blood that pours from the glass vitrine and fills the whole museum, a deep and dark red lake that is filled again and again, an aimless spring with no banks.

THE ELECTRIC PALACE
BUDAPEST, 1917
(unfolding)

It is August.

The flies, which have sucked themselves fat on apricot cakes and sugar cubes from the cafe tables, whir around my head.

And I have grown tall, my eyes flash.

My hair is shiny, my skin is shiny.

My eyelids long and dark.

My legs light and slender, swan legs.

I go lightly through the town.

The bells of the Matthias strike twelve times.

The river streams, shining and silent.

I draw gazes to myself.

Suck on my thumb, show my soft neck.

And look now, the sunrise is a fat, orange yolk bursting from the dark water, and people swim out of their houses, streaming to the marketplace under the glass roof at the end of Váci utca, their heat swelling in the blue morning air. And just look at everything that is sold here: apricots, walnuts from the orchards along the river, olives and glass jars with pickled peppers, bitter cherries, flatfish from the river that flop over the tables, and the great eels, tied up, arching.

I walk past the stalls. Dust whirls about my feet. Grease and icing drip from the stands, fume in the heat. The air is thick and flowing. Dragonflies. Potato peel, fish skins, the pulp of rotting fruit. Washing basins full of green water. A sour smell of decaying meat, blue and slimy. The sellers' eyes follow me. Sweaty faces. The gazes stick to me.

I want to taste everything, swallow everything. The sun explodes over the glass roof. The thin rays drill in under my skull. The sugar melts on my tongue, and the pots of vinegar make my eyelids crinkle. I steal a tray of quail eggs, poke holes in the dapple shells, and suck out the soft mass in my hiding spot under a chestnut tree. Curl up around my prey. Suck and suck.

The bells ring glassily in the lifts of the New York Café. The gelatinous, green light of the corridors. The sound of the tram by the zoo: the cars rattling by, the faces, moons behind the glass. The neon signs' snaking letters in the night. The voices rising and falling in the coffee houses by the river.

Women are shouting in the wash house. The sharp, whipping sounds of the blind soldiers weaving baskets outside the great gate on Dravá utca. Their blue nails. Willow twigs flutter between their fingers, and coins clink in their bowls as I pass by. Melted skin, great gaping holes in their faces. The strong scent of iodine, of their wet lamb-skin blankets, blends with the smell of thick pastry cream from the bakeries. The city's glass-blowers cast eyes for the soldiers. The soldiers cry without tears. The soldiers sing of the war, sing green gas, sing dismembered horses, sing muddy soot up to the throat, sing the Germans are coming, lopping off women's breasts, children's hands.

I have moved into the attic room above the Electric Palace. I live in Lulu's room. I lick the sunshine that falls through the skylight, that grows stronger and warmer every day. My name falls lightly from my mouth. I can turn it on my tongue like a stone under water. I walk across the courtyard, stepping lightly, the courtyard that is bathed in red light every night. It's as if the stones and the wooden beams have soaked up all that red, so they shine with neon in the daytime too. I get my sleep in small doses, like milk. Greedily I suck sleep from the night, sway between dreams and wakefulness, listen for footsteps in the courtyard, for the street dogs bounding by. On guard. I think: What if they're Tara's hounds? What if they're Tara's footsteps? What if the house calls me home, and I have to obey?

At the riverside I fetch water in big buckets, lower them into the brown water and raise them up with all my might, full of dead dragonflies, larvae, bones and ooze. I carry the buckets back to the Electric Palace and dump the water over the bar floor. In the daytime, after the night's festivities, there is always a sour stench of flesh, ammonia, absinthe. It's as if I can still hear the dancers' steps across the floor. I mimic their swaying movements. I think of Lulu. Where has she been? Who did she dance with last night?

I look for the long strands of hair she sheds everywhere, dark threads on the floor, on the windowsill.

Sweet liqueur and spit drip from the bar. I gather the empty glasses, rinse them in vinegar, blow on them and polish them with a cloth until my face appears, a warped reflection in the glass between my hands.

Iggy.

Human child.

This narrow wrist, it is mine.

I let my hand slide beneath the waistband of my trousers.

The egg is tender.

My skin cracks in tiny rifts like the skin of a ripe plum.

In the afternoons Irma and I roll in the big oval mirrors with black frames and leather handles. Then the dancers come, a little group of apprentices she practises with every day. The room comes to life: Irma covers the floor in chalk, instructs the dancers before the mirrors. They place the mirrors next to each other at a diagonal angle, so the faces are multiplied. They take their places beside the mirrors and call to each other. They bow, bend and leap over one another in turn, hang upside down from the trapezes Irma lowers from the ceiling. The dancers' laughter rises with the great clouds of talcum powder they sprinkle on their hands so they don't get blisters.

Irma says: When I dance, I dance to become someone else.

My eyes hang on the dancers like whirring dragonflies. Irma notices and laughs at me. Irma's dancers are also adorned with names: Mariska, Igor, Gizella, Ambrus. I help them get dressed, tie up their hair. They caress my cheek as if I were a child. They bathe in the big tub that Irma and I carry in to them. Their clothes cover the benches in the dressing room, where they've hastily tossed them. I can see them through the steam, the shiny skin of their faces, red and swollen in the heat, and their glistening thighs, the chests, and the little curly hairs growing under their arms. They take turns sitting in the tub, splash one another, make great swells that slosh out onto the floor. It's a flood, Irma cries, and runs over with cloths.

Why do I stay here with the dancers?

Why can't I let them go?

If I could only sit among them awhile.

If I could only.

Tantalizing necks.

Little feet.

I brush against their thighs, let them make me more real. Let them make me beautiful.

At night I find Lulu in the attic room. She sits with a book in her lap. She turns down the corners of pages, presses them carefully, so she can find every place again. It's August and the city is hot. A veiled and greasy orange light comes from the windowpane, and flies buzz lazily against the glass. Lulu reads aloud from the damp pages, slides her index finger under the letters: *those who do not move, do not notice their chains*. Her hair is in a jumble atop her forehead. She has little red marks on her throat. A pink sore like a cauliflower grows above her lips. I lean into her, run a wooden comb with broken teeth through her hair. I pull the book out of her hands. She lets me open the hard covers and feel the soft pages. I slide my finger across the letters like she does. Lulu shows me the letters, says their sounds, and I repeat the strange signs, which make my tongue wriggle and twist in my mouth. She writes:

This evening I will meet the butterflies of the night.

Lulu spits cherry stones into her hand, she has a whole pocket full of them, and the juice spreads through the fabric of her trousers. She sucks the meat from the smooth little seeds and puts them in her other pocket. Her hands, dark purple, smeared with berry juice, hold up the book.

Life sings in the sand, too, which crunches under the steps of the prison guards.

Marx, says Lulu. A copy of *Capital* slips from her hands. Have you heard of Rosa Luxemburg? Lulu laughs. Rosa, Rosa, Rosa. Rosa sings songs of freedom, against all wars, did you know that? She writes pamphlets. She's on the inside now, in prison. Before that, she lived alone, lovers visited her, they ate fried eggs and sausages. Have you seen her hair? Red Rosa's hair. It's aflame. It shines.

Lulu lights a cigarette, the smoke folds itself in arabesques over our heads. Restless wrists. Spinning and turning. Lulu has everything in her pockets. They bulge with cherry stones, with combs and seashells, her own writings. Lulu sprinkles soot from her eyes onto the sheets, sprinkles little love letters and leaflets across the floor. When I find the letters, I hide them in my breast pocket. Some nights Lulu sleeps on the mattress, but mostly she sleeps elsewhere. I long for Lulu when she isn't here, and I am happy when she comes back. I search her pockets for signs of where she's been. I find brief messages written in haste and slowly spell my way through them: *See you tomorrow. Hurry... You can find me at this address, twelve o'clock... Kút utja... Our time is much too short...* I memorize the messages, whisper them to myself, and I wish they had been written to me. *Meet me at the Liberty Bridge. I must kiss you before you fall asleep.*

I ask: What are you doing tonight?

She answers: Going to meetings.

I say: I've never been to a meeting before.

Lulu says: Irma doesn't like them. We're starting a new party. A communist party.

She shows me a printed leaflet. A great, red star.

It's a great movement.

We're going to change the world.

We're going to stop the war.

I hold a small cracked mirror up in front of her as she draws black lines under her eye with a charcoal pencil, so her eye becomes sharp as an almond.

I spread out my arms.

I am a Zeppelin.

So light.

Filled with another kind of air.

Helium, hydrogen.

A great, swaying Zeppelin with a gas flame in my throat.

Look at you.

Lulu says: I can hardly recognize you.

Since you came.

I mean, you're beautiful.

I say: Take me with you to your meeting.

I can't, not now.

Why not?

Right now it's too dangerous.

At night, when Lulu is home again, red and sleepy, she tumbles into bed, to me. Her breasts swell below her shirt. She sleeps with her clothes on. She has the city's smells with her: night smoke and liquor. Her hair clings to her forehead, her lips slightly open, eyelids quivering, her breath still blue and veiled like smoke. I can see her teeth between her lips, and I kiss her. I do it carefully, so softly, afraid she will wake up. Give her your kisses, write them across her face like her lovers' secret notes. As I kiss her, I slide into her. My winding tongue cautiously searches inside her mouth, along her hairline. Her soft lips, her heavy hair. And though I'm just a boy from the forest with a cast-off sheepskin and narrow wrists, I move closer to her, and I get so close that I'm shaking. I grow scared and want to turn away. So close that you stream into me. I am ashamed, I feel greedy. I brush a strand of hair from her forehead. I wind a lock of her dark hair around my finger. I whisper: Next time I want to come with you. She doesn't answer, only pants and sighs in her sleep. We lie entwined like two little children. Hands on thighs, cheeks, hair. We take turns rolling over beneath the moon.

The night whirls people up. I sit at the bar of the Electric Palace, bounce my foot. Red threads of light. The fog grows denser, sucks faces in, they appear again, flashing silver like fish. Arms and legs swing on the dance floor. All kinds of people come here, coffee sellers and fishermen, secretaries, seamstresses. In their work clothes. Woollen coats, light suits, leather aprons. I lick the salt from one of my fingers. Outside the bar the sign shines, THE ELECTRIC PALACE. Outside the river flows by, on the other side of the wall, mirroring everything, the water shiny, billowing silk, a ghostly presence, travellers in the night, hissing, feeding on mud, bacteria and minerals, on the riverbed and the quay, which slowly corrodes, on carp and eels, on my eyes. Like the river, I suck everything in: I want it all, everything the bar holds, the people, the sweet, thick air and the fragile voices, the open mouths, the arms shining at me like glistening trout. I want to cradle it all, swallow it.

Cigarette embers encircle me. The bar is in me like a pulsing metal box, a miniature heart.

The door opens and people slip in, a dark stripe of night outside, a feeling of water. The sharp smell of onion peel, rat shit and mould from the courtyard. The moon's ice-blue light. A lantern on the bar casts its steady red glow through the room. I feel my pulse rise.

Little Iggy. Live now. Living. Lulu comes and sits beside me. I don't want Lulu to leave, I want to hold her tight in the red circle of light around the bar. Her chest rises and falls. The red light is fabric stretched between us. Everything I might become. We are in our own time. She opens her hands.

I look at Lulu as she takes a silky-soft rolling paper from a yellow Zig-Zag pack, smooths it quickly between her fingers, licks it and rolls it up with her spiced tobacco. I want to be a part of everything Lulu is. The stream of her words. Lulu slides into drunkenness, teasingly tugs at my hair. I get burn marks on my face from the cigarettes she waves around. She gets up, disappears into the crowd, appears again up on the stage. She walks around handing out flyers, quickly pressing them onto the guests, hiding them in their coat pockets behind their backs. Lulu unfolds one of them and gives it to me. It says: *Worker*. It says: *Citizen*. It says: *Capitalism feeds on our bones*. It says: *Mass murder*. It says: *Let us put an end to the war*. It says: *Worldwide revolution*.

Aliz comes over to us. There is a veil over his eyes. He is always behind Lulu, smiling, smoking her cigarettes, flicking matches and cigarette butts onto the floor around him. His bony hands rest on my shoulders. His staccato laughter. He buys a drink. Velvet, he says, and he tells me to taste it: dark beer and champagne and then a blue blazer: whisky, lemon and sugar. Aliz throws a match down into the glass, and the liquid blazes, little transparent flames dance out over the brim, illuminate our faces from below. It looks like flowing fire, an otherworldly blue flame, as his hands pour the glowing, sticky substance from one cup to another.

I reach for the glass and drop it. Shards of glass crackle beneath my brown boots. Lulu and Aliz have vanished, but they reappear out on the dance floor. The drink sloshes in my stomach, smoky and sweet. A band on the stage, three musicians in shiny black suits, drums, guitar, harmonica. Lulu and Aliz are kissing, Lulu presses her chest against skinny Aliz, he bends down, they dig at each other, disappear into one another, the low, red light kneads their faces together.

The light splinters over our heads. The red pours from the ceiling, from the lamps, hangs in the room like mist, a fleshy, moving clump, like a freshly chopped liver.

I knot my fist, my stomach churns. Lulu and Aliz. Lulu sings in my bones, pulls long trawl nets through me.

I go out onto the dance floor too, looking for the music, for Lulu, first one step, then one more, let it fill me and caress my bones. It's easy. Easier than I thought. I hold back at first and then let go. I laugh. Get batted about. A feather, a feather in the air. Time flows out of a hole and contracts again. Smoke winds in and out among the dancers on the crowded floor. My body rocks, I move fast in my brown boots. Everyone in the room gathers by the stage, pushes up against each other, they start to dance, rhythmic, in and out of darkness, closer and closer. A heavy tone, smoke stinging my eyes. I stretch my fingers out to the crowd, I dance among them, closer than I've ever been before, eyeballs bulging. I want to dissolve into everything I see, the gestures, the twinkling, the golden stream of laughter, the faces, the tears.

I go closer to Lulu. Reach out my hand. Brush her cheek with my nails. I pull her away from Aliz, who won't let go at first, who glares at me. I whisper in her ear: Come, let's go. This, too, is easy. Easier than I thought. And yet I am burning, my bones hold my flesh together. I'm taking much too much. Lulu's hand curves into mine, and she becomes loose and warm, obedient. We don't look back. I walk with my head lifted so high I could faint. We flow through the sea of bodies, the flapping arms. Then we are outside, breathing fast and light. We stand in the court-yard, under the red light of the sign, which makes our faces smooth and luminous.

Lulu says: Wait a little.

I say: We can go this way, down to the river.

Lulu says: I need a cigarette.

I say: If only we were alone in the night.

The night is cool, a mossy fuzz. The bar, with its long dark curtains, looks deserted from outside. The river fizzes freshly. The scent of the rubbish heaps is strong, earthy and rotten. We walk down the streets, the darkness licking our ankles. The rats run towards us. Tar, oil and vinegar seep like sweat from the walls. The houses cast damp green shadows. Lamplighters in robes and long coats glide by us, bearing eggs and milk jugs, bundles of fur, bent beneath the weight.

A sharp stench of blood from the butchers' shops, blue stomachs draped over the gates like pennants. Lulu has a blister from the high-heeled shoes that are much too small for her. Blood runs from her feet and dyes her stockings. She limps along, a tent of warmth and alcoholic fumes. Lulu's cigarettes. The heat of her skin. We stand so close beneath the street lamps, soaked in blue gaslight. The bridges hang over the river. At night the city shows itself to us, the moon an egg of blood.

Come, Lulu.
Lulu giggles.

A fire like a yellow, bluepurple eye far off in the night. Down the street, a group of people circle around the flames. They are an ocean unto themselves, rocking, singing loudly, blood-red faces. *Let us fan the forge's flames ourselves, and strike while the iron is hot.* It's the Internationale, whispers Lulu. She says: Here are the butterflies of the night. Here are my friends. The flames lick at their ardent faces, eyes shining with alcohol, a rim of flesh around the fire. Some are kissing. Holding hands. Some spit, curse. We join the circle, give stern handshakes. The women wear kerchiefs. The women know Lulu, hug her, pinch her cheeks. The flames lick, words fill the air.

The revolution.

The revolution in the Russian February.
Blue from the cold. The tsar deposed.
The Bolshevik uprising. Soviet.

The people around the fire use the same words as Lulu. They pass around a bowl with soft goat's cheese, sauerkraut, bread, a bottle of sweet wine. The cheese, fresh and thick and good, drips from my lips. The wine is so sweet it makes me nauseous. The bottle goes from hand to hand, and we share each other's spit.

They say: Come here and be here with us. We nod. We want to be with them. I'm drunk, drunk on Lulu, on the intense heat, on the night that opens like an endless field of heavy, green wheat. They sing again when the fire collapses and sinks into a blue clearing. Lulu takes my hand, right in front of everyone she kisses me.

The red of the flames presses into my eyes, orange, blue, flows deep into my brain like a glowing drink. Sparks whirl over the rooftops. Then the voices rise around us, mutters and shouts, someone gets angry, someone throws a punch. Come, says Lulu, we can't stay here.

I grow calm when we get down to the quay, my body stretches towards the water, thick as oil, I lick it up. Metallic clicks from the fishing boats. We follow the bends of the river. The surface slowly rises and falls in great, soft swells. We scramble up and down the bank, look down at the whirling water. The fresh and sweet, dizzying smell I know so well rams into me. Algae and iron-green scum. I crouch down and take off my boots, shake off my clothes, my coat, my trousers, and I take a step out into the water.

The surface is ruffled, cold and metallic, but as soon as I put my head under I feel the warm current, the strong sucking of the water around my body. The eels suck the soles of my feet. Lulu follows me, puts her clothes on the quay and slides down into the river. The water wakes us. The current is strong, the city twinkles high above, threads of cigarette smoke, voices along the banks. Here, the city becomes strange again, a place I have never been, never even visited.

The water and the sky are white. Light flutters on the horizon. We crawl out of the river and lie close together at the edge of the quay, sleepy puppies, huddled together, the warmth of our faces flows out, radioactive. I stretch so I can feel every single tendon in my body tighten against my skin. The stones scrape our naked backs. The sun's first orange embers are scattered on our bellies.

Lulu holds my hands, turns them in hers. I lay my head on her belly, listen to its bubbling. She smells of clay, of smoke, the tallow in her hair. Lulu lies on top of me, rests her fingers on my flat, scarred chest. My deep belly button. Her fingers leave behind spots of coal dust and blood. Lulu sticks her fingers into the dark hollows where my nipples were, counts my ribs, caresses the scar tissue, the hard, horned layer of skin. Lulu's spit tastes sour. We are gentle, we are sharp, we bite each other. I unfold myself beneath Lulu's body. I lick her ears.

We lie on top of each other without falling, perfectly balanced. My egg is swollen, and I tremble. Lulu puts her hand over it, right where I want it to be, rubs in soft movements with her thumb and index finger, so gentle I can hardly feel it, and yet every movement flows up to the tip of my spine, through the curled threads of my nerves. Her mouth is slightly open. I feel her soft breasts against my ribs. I press my lips against her forehead. We giggle. My fingers find their way over her belly. There is a hollow in Lulu, in all bodies, an entrance to a world. The hollow sings blood and life and spit and flaking skin. I arch my back, Lulu lays her hand on my belly, presses her nails between my thighs.

BLEGDAM HOSPITAL
COPENHAGEN, 1952
(December)

I am not surprised when the night flyers come. I call to them, and they come back, night after night. They are a great grey cloud. There are so many that they darken the room. They land on the hands of the clock, which stops. They crawl on the inner side of the iron lung. The walls come to life. They flap about me, crawl over my breast and into my nose, down my throat. They crawl around inside my lungs, tickle my trachea. The insects blow out of my mouth when I speak. The night flyers' minute movements linger in the room like an echo after they've gone. Then they return with a new force. They make the room writhe, dark and soft and beaming. They are inside me. They lift me up. I've never been so alive before. I blink. The night flyers flap towards the fans of the ventilators.

Agnes?

    Agnes?

Mother is leaning over me.

    Mother says: I hardly recognize you.

    Mother spits in her hand and wipes my forehead, where my eyebrows have grown together.

I say: Mother, why didn't you tell me I'll never walk again?

    Mother says: You shouldn't believe everything the doctors say.

    I say: Am I very sick?

    Mother says: You need more examinations. You've got to stay here. They can't let you out.

    I say: Mother, I want to travel. Can't we travel abroad?

    Mother rubs my hand. Nods. Yes. But not now. First you need a little more rest.

Those who are dying in the machine say that it's like drowning. That they're sinking and sinking in a bottomless sea.

Now the soul factory, the great hospital, is empty. The beds in the epidemic wing are made up, their tight white sheets gaping, waiting for the next patients to come. The infection rate has fallen. The ward always has the most patients in the summertime, but now it is winter, and the snow has started falling soft and white outside, covering the hospital gardens. Berries shine red on the hedges. The nurses' footsteps echo in the great hall. The doctors walk up and down the corridors in their white coats, signing patient records, releasing the ones who are better.

They roll me into my own room. Silence is braided among the white metal bars.

Soon I'm the only one left, all the other children have either died or got well enough to go home. The doctor comes into my room, reads my records. Mother, by my side, squeezes her hands together, seals off her face to keep from crying. The doctor says that they need to keep me under observation for a few more months, that I need to learn to breathe on my own again, but it's going too slowly to continue the training without the iron lung, they have to wait and see. One by one the other machines are rolled out of the hall, and I am left behind with the creaky breathing of the iron lung.

In the beginning I said to Ella: Tell me about Copenhagen. Tell me about the weather. About the smells. About the people. About the twelve strikes of the town hall clock.

Ella said: I rode my bicycle along the reservoir, right by the edge.

Ella said: I watched the boys. They walked by the water in a little group. They stayed close together. Pretty faces. School bags swinging. Pomade and grease in their hair, sun in their skin. The sun sprawled across their backs. Then they ran.

Later, Ella said: I stood by the reservoir, the water was so clear. The chestnut trees were all bare. I tossed a stone into the water. It went bloop. I had one hand under my blouse. I was thinking of him, my love.

Later, she said: Agnes, it's so stupid not to be friends. I bought you some dried figs. Try them. You're my sister, for goodness' sake. My silly little sister. I just want us to forget about everything. Everything.

I watched Ella for a long time. I told her to stand still before the iron lung's mirror, so I could see the shadows of the world I've left behind. I couldn't get enough of the smells hanging around her: the smell of fried food from the cafeteria, the smell of vanilla from her milkshake and the liquorice she brought with her, which we shared. But it no longer interests me. I turn towards myself, I fold myself into myself, I close my eyes.

Every now and then, when the nurses take me out of the machine to wash me or examine me, I cry, and I ask them to put me back in. I don't calm down until they've laid me down on the stretcher and pushed me into the iron lung, until I hear the machinery whirring and the pressure embraces my lungs.

I call the machine Mother. I sing with it, stroke my left hand across its smooth sheath, scratch the iron shell with my nails. I listen to all its sounds, its creaking and sighing and panting. When it sleeps, I sleep, and I wake with it. I call to the iron lung in my dreams. The machine is always here, it is all I have, and it holds me gently, peels layer after layer off me, off my body, which is now a mere husk, without blood, without muscles, off my life, which appears only in quick flashes, the house, the soft green lawn beneath my bare feet, Mother's dry hands, the sweet smell of her Nivea cream, before it all disappears again, and the only thing I want to do is stretch my arms and walk through a big room full of light and air. But now I am here. I no longer believe I will walk again upon the light green grass or feel its long, feathery blades tickle the soles of my feet. In this silence I am free. I have surrendered myself entirely to the iron lung, which dispenses its love to me calmly, steadily, strokes my belly with its cool air. The machine lives on electricity and my breath, it wraps itself around me, never rests, gives me everything I need to live. My milk is the oxygen that is pumped in and out, that swirls around my chest, through the iron wombshell. I am born in the machine, and I will never abandon it. I am in the machine, which moves me, which kneads my chest, and its every movement pushes me closer to the light, to a new time. A time when I can walk out of my body and into another. My whole body is so light. I live in the machine. I float in the machine. I am filled with its love.

Last night I lay awake. I looked out through the garden and into one of the other buildings. I saw a light. There was only one girl in the whole ward. The room was so brightly illuminated. The girl was thin, like me, and she wore a hospital gown with short sleeves and blue stripes. She lay in her bed. Beside her was an apple on a little wheeled table, so perfect and red and round in the sharp light that it looked artificial, like a piece of soap. She could lift herself part way up, and she waved to me and smiled. She shaped her mouth into a question. I think she asked my name.

Iggy, I whispered. I waved back.

August is the hottest month. Flies hang in clusters down by the river, the water bubbles and foams green. The heavy, monotonous summer rain makes the river swell. Farther up the river, the water runs over the banks and floods the fields, spongy and iron-green. The newspaper hawkers yell loudest and shrillest. Their shouts linger high over Budapest in the still air. The chestnut trees and lime trees rustle in the rain. Spit lies thick on the cobblestones, and all manner of illnesses flourish in the heavy air: diphtheria, tuberculosis, typhus, which the soldiers bring back from the front. The spit covers the leaflets that are passed from hand to hand: *The next great moment in history belongs to us. In the darkness, I smile at life. No war, but revolution.*

My skin is thin and cracks easily, as if there is no longer any membrane between me and the world. When Lulu kisses me, I get raw around my mouth. Her fingerprints are on my back, my throat. Lulu sweeps away my dry skin. She throws the big, wrinkled flakes I shed in a long trail to the pigeons in the courtyard. She rubs me down with lard and beeswax. Strokes my chest with a long, soft leather whip. Rubs and massages until I gleam like a cake covered in thick icing.

In Budapest the hours are still. The attic is soft and dark. I walk through the door, across the floorboards, lean over the sofa. I lie down beside Lulu, sink my nose into her hair. Talcum powder, oil, smoke. Strands of hair stick to my mouth. Later, we go out. Later, we loosen ourselves from the darkness, slosh out of it as if from an egg white. We move through the night, hand in hand. Lazy and light. We follow the river. The water smells fresh, sweet as our fingers. The men of Budapest call after us, they latch on to us for a way, only to let go again, swaying, spitting, cigarette embers circling, but we keep on walking, brash, so audacious we could just die, laughing, along the river, into the night.

NOTES

Works of special significance to the writing of *Iron Lung*:

Anita Kurimay, *Queer Budapest, 1873–1961*. The University of Chicago Press, 2020.

Katrine Nielsen (ed.), *Mit liv med polio: En antologi af livsberetninger* ['My life with polio: an anthology of recollections']. PolioForeningen, 2011.

Jim B. Tucker, *Life Before Life: Children's Memories of Previous Lives*. St Martin's Press, 2005.

Paul Warwicker, *Polio: historien om den store polioepidemi i København i 1952* ['Polio: the story of the great polio epidemic of 1952']. Gyldendal, 2006.

Epidemien: jeg husker ikke noget, men jeg glemmer det aldrig ['Epidemic: I Can't Remember a Thing, but I'll Never Forget It'] (film), director and screenwriter: Niels Frandsen, Niels Frandsens Productions, 2001.

Citations:

Page 82: *The god of time, Chronos, is the father of Chaos.*
The sisters have learned about Chronos from Orphism.
The Orphics devised their own teachings about the origin
of the world.

Page 110: *O little frog, I'm taking you, quack-quack,
quack-quack, quack-quack.* 'En lille frø i mosen sad' ['A
little frog sat in the bog']. Song lyrics by Anna Wulff;
translation by Hunter Simpson.

Page 248: *Let us fan the forge's flames ourselves, and
strike while the iron is hot.* The Internationale, socialist
song, written in 1871. Eugène Pottier, *Chants révolu-
tionnaires*. Dentu, 1887. Translation by Mitchell Abidor,
marxists.org.

Page 264: *The next great moment in history belongs to
us.* The sentence is from *Skarpretteren* ['The executioner']
(film), written and directed by Ursula Reuter Christiansen,
1972. Translation by Hunter Simpson.

Page 264: *In the darkness, I smile at life.* Rosa Luxemburg,
Briefe aus dem Gefängnis ['Letters from prison']. Verlag
der Jugendinternationale, 1922. Translation by Hunter
Simpson.

ACKNOWLEDGEMENTS

Thank you to everyone who read drafts of *Iron Lung* as the book was being written, and special thanks to: Øyvind Ellenes, Aina Villanger, Ditte Holm Bro, Liv Nimand Duvå, Laima Nomeikaite, Kristine Friis Jensen, Merete Enggaard Jakobsen, Sara Sølberg, Siri Katinka Valdez and Liv Kristin Holmberg.

Iron Lung is dedicated to Laima and Anais.

THE PEIRENE SUBSCRIPTION

Since 2011, Peirene Press has run a subscription service which has brought a world of translated literature to thousands of readers. We seek out great stories and original writing from across the globe, and work with the best translators to bring these books into English – before sending each one to our subscribers ahead of publication. All of our books are beautifully designed collectible paperback editions, printed in the UK using sustainable materials.

Join our reading community today and subscribe to receive three or six books a year, as well as invitations to events and launch parties and discounts on all our titles. We also offer a gift subscription, so you can share your literary discoveries with friends and family.

A one-year subscription costs £38 for three books, or £68 for six books. Postage costs apply.

www.peirenepress.com/subscribe

'The foreign literature specialist'

The Sunday Times

'A class act'

The Guardian